The Riddle

That
Never
Was

Enid Blyton

The Riddle

That Never Was

PART OF THE RIDDLES SERIES

Bounty
Books

This edition published in 2015 by Bounty Books,
a division of Octopus Publishing Group Ltd
Carmelite House,
50 Victoria Embankment,
London EC4Y 0DZ
www.octopusbooks.co.uk

An Hachette UK Company
www.hachette.co.uk

First published 1961 as *The Mystery That Never Was*.
Revised edition published 1997 as *The Riddle That Never Was*

ENID BLYTON ® Text copyright © 1961, 2013 Hodder & Stoughton Ltd.
Illustrations copyright © Octopus Publishing Group Ltd, 2015
Layout copyright © Octopus Publishing Group Ltd, 2015

Illustrated by Patricia Ludlow
Cover illustration by David Frankland

ISBN: 978-0-75372-547-4

A CIP catalogue record for this book is available from the British Library

Printed and bound in the United Kingdom

Contents

Chapter 1

News at Breakfast-Time

Nick Terry came down the stairs at top speed, his dog Punch at his heels, barking in excitement. The little terrier flung himself against the kitchen door and it flew open, crashing against the wall.

The family were having breakfast. Nick's father gave a roar of anger. "Nick! What's the matter with you this morning? Take that dog out of the room!"

Mrs Terry put down her coffee mug and fended off Punch, who was leaping up joyfully at her. Nick's grandmother, who had lived with the Terrys since her husband, Nick's grandfather, had died, smiled at him. She tapped her son on the hand.

"Just like you used to be when you were his age!" she said.

"Hi, everyone!" said Nick, beaming round

as he helped himself to scrambled eggs. "Did you all sleep well?"

"Get that dog off my feet!" said his father.

"Come here, Punch, and have a bit of bacon," called Nick. "I don't think Dad can have slept very well last night, do you?"

"Don't give that dog titbits," said Nick's father, "and will you take him—"

"—out of the room!" finished Nick. He put his plate down on the table and turned to give his father a sudden hug. "Oh, Dad – it's a wonderful sunny day, Mike's back from his holiday, Katie's coming home next week and there's still a fortnight left before the autumn term starts!"

"I don't know whether I can cope with another two weeks of noise," said his father, laughing. "Stop watching me eat, Punch – you know I don't feed dogs at the table!"

Punch removed himself and went to sit on Gran's feet. He gave her leg a long lick. He loved her very much. She never shouted at him!

"I suppose you and Mike have plenty of plans for the rest of the holidays?" said the old lady. "It's lucky he lives next door."

"Actually," said Nick, buttering his toast, "we haven't any definite plans. We thought we'd teach Punch a few more tricks, like fetching shoes or slippers for people. Gran, wouldn't you be pleased if Punch fetched you your slippers to put on, when you came in from a walk?"

"Good heavens!" said his father. "Don't tell me we're going to find slippers strewn about all over the place!"

"What's that dog eating?" said Mrs Terry, as a loud crunching noise came from under the table. "Oh Nick, you've given him a piece of toast again."

"I bet it was Gran who gave it to him," said Nick. "Punch, stop eating so rudely. I think he'll be much quicker learning tricks now than he was at Easter, Dad."

"Yes, yes, yes," said his father. "Now, be quiet! I want to read the paper, and your mother hasn't even read her letters yet."

Mrs Terry was reading a short letter. Nick's sharp eyes immediately recognised the handwriting.

"I bet that's from Uncle Bob!" he said. "Has he had any exciting jobs lately, Mum?"

"Yes, it is from your Uncle Bob," said his mother, putting down the letter. "He's coming to stay with us for a while, and—"

"Great!" cried Nick, putting his mug down with a thump. "Did you hear that, Punch?"

Punch barked joyfully, and came out from under the table, his tail thumping against Mr Terry's leg. He was promptly pushed back again.

"Mum! I say, Mum, he isn't coming down here on a job, is he?" asked Nick, his eyes shining. "I bet he is! Mum, will he do some investigating here? I'll help him, if so. Mike will too. What's the job? Is it something we—?"

"Nick! Don't get so excited!" said his mother. "No. Uncle Bob is coming down here because he's been ill and wants a rest."

"Oh, bother! I thought he might be hunting a murderer or a swindler or a – a kidnapper or something," said Nick, disappointed. "I'm the only boy at school whose uncle is a detective, Mum. I know he's only my godfather and not a real uncle but nobody else knows that."

"Uncle Bob's a private investigator," his

mother corrected him. "His work is—"

"Oh, I know all about his work," said Nick, taking another piece of toast. "They've got plenty of investigators on television. Last week one had a really difficult case to solve. It ended up in an aeroplane chase, and—"

"You watch too much television," said his father, gathering up his letters. "And now, listen to me, Nick! If Bob is coming here for a rest, he will not want hordes of gaping schoolboys coming here to listen to his adventures! Bob is not supposed to talk about them anyway – they're private. Nobody is to be told that he's the uncle you've been boasting about."

"Oh Dad, can't I even tell Mike?" said Nick in dismay.

"Well, I suppose you can't possibly keep anything from Mike," said his father, going out of the room. "But only Mike, mind!"

"I shall tell him immediately after breakfast!" said Nick, passing another bit of toast under the table. "Did you hear the news, Punch? Wow, we'll have some fun with Uncle Bob! Mum, have you ever seen him in any of his disguises? Can I ask him to come in disguise tomorrow, to see if Mike and I can spot him?"

"Oh, don't be so ridiculous, Nick," said his mother. "And listen, there's to be no going over to Mike's until you've tidied up your room. All your things seem to be spread over the floor!"

"Okay, Mum!" said Nick. "Come on, Punch. You're going to be busy in the next few weeks, learning a whole lot of new tricks! That's the time to learn, you know, when you're young! And you're hardly a year old yet. Scram!"

Punch scrammed. He shot out into the hall, sending the mat flying, and ran up the stairs, barking. He bounded into Nick's room and raced round and round the bed at top speed, still barking madly. Oh, what joy to have Nick all day long!

Mrs Terry gave a sigh of relief to see the back of them both. When his sister was away, Nick seemed to be permanently over the top; Katie definitely had a calming influence on him.

In his bedroom, Nick picked up all his scattered clothes and stuffed them into his drawers.

"There, that's done, Punch," he said, patting him. "Now to phone Uncle Bob."

He crept downstairs to the study. No one seemed to be about. He went in, shut the door and sat down by the telephone.

He rang Uncle Bob's number and waited impatiently, Punch sitting as close to him as possible.

His uncle's secretary answered.

"Oh, is that you, Mrs Hewitt?" said Nick. "It's Nick Terry here. Now, you know Uncle Bob's coming to stay with us tomorrow?

Could you tell him I'll meet him with my friend Mike, and we'd like him to come in disguise just to see if we can spot him. You won't forget, will you?"

"I'll tell him," said the voice at the other end of the phone. "That's if I see him before he leaves but it may be that I..."

Nick heard footsteps approaching along the hall, said goodbye hurriedly, and put down the telephone. He couldn't help feeling that his father would consider it a waste of money to use the telephone to ask Uncle Bob such a thing. Luckily the footsteps passed the study door, and Nick crept out unseen.

"Come on, Punch! We'll go and find Mike and tell him Uncle Bob's coming!" he said to the excited dog. "Race you out into the garden! Go!"

Chapter 2

Down in the Shed

Punch took the short cut that the boys always used, out of the back door, through the yard and down the garden to the hole in the hedge. Mrs Hawes, their home help, shook her broom at Punch as he flew past, almost tripping her up.

"You and that boy!" she said. "Sixty miles an hour and no brakes! Give me a cat any time!"

Punch and Nick squeezed through the hole in the yew hedge, and Nick gave a piercing whistle. It was immediately answered by Mike, who was down in his garden shed, looking after his adored mice. Punch arrived there before Nick and flung himself on Mike whom, after Nick and Katie, he loved with all his heart. He licked him from top to toe, giving little whines all the time.

"You'll wear your tongue out, Punch!" said Mike. "Stop it now. I've already washed twice this morning. What a dog! Hello, Nick! I see Punch is his usual crazy self. Hope you are too!"

Nicked grinned. "Hello, Mike! Did you have a brilliant holiday? We did. We went mackerel fishing at night, and sailed a three-metre dinghy during the day. It was great! How are your mice?"

"Fine. I've just finished feeding them," said Mike. "Look at this tiddler – the youngest of the lot, and the cutest. Get down, Punch. He's an awfully nosy dog, isn't he, Nick? Nosy would be a much better name for him than Punch."

"Listen, Mike, I've a bit of news," said Nick, pulling Punch away from the cage. "Wait a minute, though, where's that nosy sister of yours? She's not anywhere about, is she?"

"She might be," said Mike cautiously, and went to the door of the shed to see if his sister Penelope was in sight. "No, all clear," he said, and came back.

"Penny's just about as nosy as Punch,"

said Nick. "Listen, Mike, you know my Uncle Bob, Dad's best friend who's my godfather, the one who's a sort of detective?"

"Yes – what about him? Has he solved some mystery or other?" said Mike, interested at once. "I say, did you watch that detective show last night, where nobody could make out who stole the—?"

"No, I didn't. Do listen, Mike. Uncle Bob is arriving tomorrow, so I phoned him and asked him to come in disguise. Then we can show him how good we are at tracking people and seeing through any disguise. Uncle Bob's brilliant at disguising himself. He showed me his special wardrobe once, full of all kinds of different clothes and hats! You should have seen them!"

"Wow!" said Mike. "Do you think he's coming down to do some detective work here in our town? Can we help him? We're not bad at disguises ourselves, are we? Do you remember that time when you dressed up as a guy and I wheeled you round the town just before Guy Fawkes Night? If you hadn't had a coughing fit, nobody would ever have seen through that disguise!"

"Mum says he's not coming to do any detecting here," said Nick mournfully. "But, of course, he might not have told her if anything was up. He's supposed to be coming because he needs a rest."

"That's a likely story!" said Mike scornfully. "I never in my life saw anyone so bursting with health as your Uncle Bob. The way he made us walk for miles, too, do you remember? Personally, I'm quite glad to hear he needs a rest!"

"Well, anyway, he's coming tomorrow," said Nick. "And, as I said, I asked if he'd come in disguise. He's always one for a joke, you know, so what disguise do you think he'll wear?"

There was a pause. Mike scratched his head. "Well, he might dress up as an old man," he said.

"Yes, he might," said Nick. "Or as a postman. I saw a postman's jacket in his wardrobe. Anyway, there's one thing he can't disguise, and that's his big feet!"

"Would he disguise himself as a woman?" asked Mike.

"I don't think so; the voice would be

difficult," said Nick, considering the matter. "And the walk, too. Uncle Bob's got a proper man's walk."

"Well, so has Penny's riding teacher," pointed out Mike. "And her voice is really deep. Like this!"

And to Punch's alarmed surprise he suddenly spoke in a curious, deep-down, hoarse voice. Punch growled at once.

"It's all right, Punch." Nick grinned, patting him. "That was terrific, Mike. Well, what we'll do is go to the station and meet the London train with old Punch here, and—"

"But that wouldn't be fair," objected Mike. "Punch would recognise him at once by the smell. We'd better leave him behind. He'd do what he always does when he sees or smells anyone he knows, go round them in circles, barking his head off."

"Yes, you're right. We won't take Punch then," said Nick. "He'll be really upset, though. We'll lock him in your shed."

"No. He'll howl the place down," said Mike. "Lock him in yours."

"Okay," said Nick. "Do you hear that, Punch? In the shed for you tomorrow while we go out, and if you don't make a sound, I'll give you an enormous bone."

"Woof." said Punch, wagging his tail violently at the word "bone". The boys patted him, and he rolled over on his back, doing his favourite bicycling act with all four legs in the air.

"Daft dog," said Nick. "What shall we do today, Mike?"

"Shhh!" said Mike, as the sound of someone singing came up the path. "There's Penny. Pretend to be tidying up the shed in case she wants us to do anything."

At once the two boys began to pull boxes about feverishly, and straighten up things on the dirty shelves. A face peered in at the door.

"Oh, so there you are," said Penny, and came right into the shed. "Did you have a good holiday, Nick? Where's Katie?"

"We had a wonderful time. We made friends with twins called Sophie and David who were staying next door to us. They're redheads and great fun," replied Nick. "Katie went back to stay with Sophie for a few days because David was going camping with the Scouts."

"When's she coming back?" asked Penny.

"Sometime next week," said Nick. "She's looking forward to seeing you again."

"Good," said Penny. "I've lots to tell her. Incidentally, Mike, you've been such an age feeding your mice that Mum wondered what on earth you were up to."

"You mean *you* did!" said Mike, busily brushing a great deal of dust off a shelf, all over Penny. "Look out! We're busy, as you can see. Like to help? It's a pretty dirty job, though, cleaning out this shed."

"Well! I've never seen you clean out this shed before!" said Penny, sneezing as the dust flew around. "I came to see if you'd help me mend my bicycle brake. It's gone again."

"Penny, we're busy!" said Mike. "I'll do it tonight. Or you can ask the gardener if he'll help you. He's good at bikes."

"Well, I certainly don't want to stay here in this mess and muddle!" said Penny. "Get down, Punch. Look how you've dirtied me with your paws!"

"Oh, get lost!" said Mike, and swished another cloud of dust from a nearby shelf. Penny sneezed again, and hurried out.

Nick looked at Mike. "Shall I go and help her?" he said. "She just might have an accident, you know. We've plenty of time."

"I can hear her asking the gardener," said Mike, climbing down from the box he was standing on. "She's a nosy parker and she only came down to see what we were doing! Why are girls so nosy?"

"Katie's not nosy like Penny," said Nick. "We tell each other most things, and I miss her when she's away. I shouldn't like to be on my own all the time. Still, I've always got Punch, I suppose!"

"Woof!" said Punch, and licked his hand.

Mike looked round the shed. "We might as well clean it up properly now," he said. "We've nothing to do till tomorrow when Uncle Bob arrives. Won't we get filthy!"

They worked hard, and quite enjoyed themselves. "Gosh, we're a sight!" said Nick. "I'd better go in and change, and hope I don't bump into Mum on the way. Then tomorrow we'll show Uncle Bob that we can see through any disguise he puts on! Come on, Punch, lunch-time!"

Chapter 3

Which is Uncle Bob?

The next day the two boys left a very angry Punch locked up in Nick's shed. "Hope Penny won't hear him howling and let him out," said Mike. "Hey, I'd better come home with you and give my hair a brush. If I go into my house and Mum sees me I might be sent on all kinds of errands."

"Well, come on in," said Nick. "Back way, then we'll only see Mrs Hawes."

Nick put on a clean shirt and washed his face, while Mike brushed his hair vigorously. Through the open window came woeful howls from the garden shed. Poor Punch!

"Now to slip out without Mum seeing us," said Nick. "I don't want to have to stop and do odd jobs just as we're off to meet the train."

They crept down the stairs and made

for the kitchen again. An astonished voice called after them: "Oh! There you are, Nick! I wanted you to—"

"Sorry, Mum – we're off to meet the London train!" shouted Nick. "Uncle Bob, you know!"

"Yes, but wait, Nick, you silly boy, you won't be..." began his mother, coming out of the sitting-room after them. But the boys had disappeared, and the kitchen door banged.

"Narrow escape!" panted Nick, racing round to the front gate. "Come on! We'll just get to the station in time."

The train was signalled as they ran on to the platform. "Now you keep a watch on the people coming from the back of the train, and I'll watch the front," said Nick. "And remember to look for big feet!"

Mike remembered quite well what Nick's Uncle Bob looked like; a tall man with black hair, keen eyes and a determined mouth. "Still, he might wear a false moustache or a beard this morning," thought Mike. "And stand bent over like an old man." He stood waiting as the train came in and pulled to a stop.

Six people stepped down from the carriages. Two were women, both small. They could be ruled out at once. One was a boy, who went whistling down the platform. That left three. Nick and Mike looked at them closely.

An oldish man with a beard was shuffling along, head poking forward, glasses on his nose – and he had large feet! Nick brightened up at once. "Might quite well be Uncle Bob!" he thought, and fell in behind him.

Of the other two, one was a postman with a big bag. He too had large feet, and was bent under the weight of his heavy load. He had a small moustache, and he mopped his face with a handkerchief as he went, giving an explosive sneeze as he passed the boys. They nudged one another.

"Bet that's him!" whispered Mike. "You follow him and I'll follow the old man, just in case! I don't think that other person's any good. Small feet!"

Nick nodded. He followed closely behind the postman, wishing he could get a better look at him. Yes, he definitely had large feet! Nick tried to peer into his face as he walked past him, but the man was still mopping his nose. He slung his bag from one shoulder to the other, and it knocked against Nick.

"Hey!" said Nick, almost bowled over by the weight of the bag. "Got a cold, Uncle Bob?"

"What are you following me about for?" growled the postman. "Think you're being funny calling me uncle? Clear off."

His voice was not deep, but rather hoarse as if he had a bad cold. Nick decided that it was definitely a false voice. He gave the postman a nudge. "Come on, Uncle Bob! Own up! I'd know your voice anywhere, even though you're making it as croaky as an old crow's. But it's a jolly good disguise!"

The postman put his bag down with a thump and glared at Nick, who now saw the man's whole face very clearly. It was nothing like his Uncle Bob's and the little moustache was obviously real! Nick began to feel most uncomfortable.

"Sorry!" he said, awkwardly. "I just thought you were – er – in disguise, you know. I was looking for someone else!"

"Now, you clear off, see? And if my

voice sounds like an old crow's, so would yours with a cold like mine," said the angry postman, and sneezed again so violently that his cap almost flew off.

"It was a mistake," said poor Nick, red in the face. "I apologise!" And he raced off after Mike, who was still following the old man. Mike was lucky, thought Nick, that must be Uncle Bob, shuffling along, pulling at his beard and mumbling to himself.

He caught up with Mike and raised his eyebrows, muttering, "Any luck?"

Mike nodded. "I think so. Haven't said anything yet, though. Look at his feet!"

Nick looked. Yes, they were just about the same size as Uncle Bob's, and so were his hands. That beard was clever, it hid half the face! The old man suddenly stopped, pulled out a packet of cigarettes and lit one, holding the match with trembling fingers. He flipped the match away with finger and thumb. "Just like Uncle Bob always does!" thought Nick. "Good, I'll have a little fun with you!"

So he fell into step beside the old man and began to talk. "Do you know the way to Mr Terry's house?" he asked, and Mike gave a grin, for that, of course was Nick's home. "I'll take you there myself, if you like."

"Don't play the fool," grunted the old man in a husky voice. "What are you two boys following me for?"

"What big feet you've got, Uncle Bob!" said Nick. "And do let me feel your nice thick beard!"

The old man looked angry and a little frightened. He walked on, saying nothing, then suddenly crossed the road to where the town policeman stood, stolid and burly.

"Constable, will you take these boys' names, and tell their parents they have been harassing me?" said the old man. The policeman stared in astonishment at Nick and Mike, whom he knew well.

"Now what have you two been doing to old Mr Holdsworth?" he demanded. Then he turned back to the old man. "All right, sir," he said. "I'll deal with this for you. Young rascals!"

"Is he really an old man?" said Nick, taken aback, as he watched the old fellow go off, mumbling. "I thought he was my Uncle Bob in disguise. Is he really Mr Holdsworth?"

"Now look here, Nick Terry, you know he's an old man all right, and no more your Uncle Bob than I am!" said the policeman. "Don't you start getting into trouble like some of the youngsters in this town! Playing the fool and making fun of old people isn't the sort of thing your parents would like to hear about."

"It was a mistake, really it was," stammered poor Nick, and Mike nodded his head too, scared. "You see..."

"Go home," said the policeman impatiently. "I've no time to waste on silly

kids that don't act their age. Next time I'll deal with you properly."

He marched out into the road and began sorting out a small traffic jam. The two boys, red in the face, hurried home. They felt very foolish indeed.

Nick saw his mother in the front garden and yelled to her. "Mum! We went to meet Uncle Bob, and he wasn't on the train."

"Well, no wonder!" said his mother. "Didn't you hear what I called out to you, when you left in such a hurry? I said he was coming by car!"

"Oh no!" said both boys at once. Nick groaned. "Gosh – what idiots we've been! What time is Uncle Bob arriving, then?"

At that moment a sports car drew up in front of the house, and the horn was blown loudly. The boys swung round.

"It's Uncle Bob! Uncle Bob, we've been meeting several of you at the station! What a smashing car! Come on in, you're just in time for lunch!"

Chapter 4

Good Old Uncle Bob!

Uncle Bob was just the same as ever, except that he was a bit thinner, and rather pale. Nick's mother made a fuss of him.

"Oh, Bob! Whatever have you been doing to yourself? You're as thin as a rake!"

"Now, Lucy, don't exaggerate!" said Uncle Bob, and gave her such a bear-hug that she gasped. "I'm a bit overdone, that's all! If you can put up with me for a week or two, I'll soon be as fit as a fiddle! Hello, boys, what's this about meeting several of me at the station?"

During lunch, the boys told him about following the postman and the old man, thinking that they were Uncle Bob in disguise, and he roared with laughter.

"You are a couple of idiots! I can see you need a few lessons in detective work! Come on upstairs and help me to unpack my bags."

It was great to have Uncle Bob staying with them again. Punch was delighted too. When the boys let him out of the shed, giving him a bone as they'd promised, he ignored the bone completely and tore up the garden, barking loudly. He'd already heard Uncle Bob's voice, and not even a juicy bone could tempt him! He flung himself on Uncle Bob, and licked every bit of him that he could.

"Here, be careful of Uncle Bob, he's rather frail at the moment," said Nick, grinning. "Isn't he pleased to see you, Uncle! I'm glad you've come now because we've still got nearly two weeks of the holidays left."

"Good!" said Uncle Bob, clapping Nick on the back. "You'll be able to take me for some walks, and maybe we can do some bird-watching. You're still interested in birds, I suppose?"

"Oh yes," said Nick, pleased. "Mike and I plan to go out bird-watching as usual. We've heard there's a sparrow-hawk somewhere on the hills, and we'd like to find out where it nested. Mike's got an old pair of binoculars. Wish I had!"

"Well, I might lend you my pair," said his uncle, opening his bag. "I always have a pair with me, useful in my work, you know, and as I shan't be needing them this time, I could lend them to you. That's if you promise to care for them as if they were made of gold! They're very good ones."

"Oh, Uncle Bob! Thanks a million!" said Nick, overjoyed. "It's not much fun sharing a pair, you know. Mike always wants to use them when I'm longing to, though it's great of him to lend them to me, anyhow. Now we'll each have a pair. Are these the ones you use? What fantastic binoculars! I bet Mum'll say you're not to lend them to me!"

"And where's Katie?" asked Uncle Bob, changing the subject.

"She's staying with friends we made on holiday in Swanage," answered Nick. "You'll see her next week."

After they'd finished Uncle Bob's unpacking, they all walked down to the town to buy some toothpaste as Uncle Bob had forgotten to bring any.

"I'm going to sit down and have a look at the paper," said Uncle Bob when they got back home. "I don't seem to have a great deal of energy at the moment."

"Poor Uncle Bob," said Mike as he said goodbye to Nick. "I hope he feels better soon. He's normally such good fun!"

"Yes, everyone likes him," said Nick. "Mrs Hawes can't do enough for him."

Uncle Bob was fast asleep in his chair when tea was ready. Nick was sent to wake him up.

"I hope you're feeling a little bit hungry, Bob," said Mum, cutting into a large cake. "I know you like fruitcakes."

"We always have great food when you come to stay," said Nick, eyeing the cake. "I bet we'll get heaps of cakes now, because Uncle Bob likes them, won't we Mum?"

"Everyone always spoils Bob," said his mother, laughing.

"I wish I was spoilt," said Nick. "How do you manage it, Uncle Bob?"

"Let's change the subject," said his godfather.

"I'm going to teach Punch a whole lot of new tricks. Would you help me?" asked Nick.

"You bet," said Uncle Bob, helping himself to a second piece of the fruitcake.

"Heavens, Lucy, with cakes like this, I shall soon have trouble buttoning my shirts!"

Punch was sitting as close to Uncle Bob as he could. He liked his smell. He liked his voice. He liked the firm way in which Uncle Bob patted his head and he loved the exciting long walks they always went on when Uncle Bob came to stay.

"I thought I'd teach Punch to fetch people's slippers for them," said Nick. "Think how pleased Dad would be to find his slippers by his armchair each night! And I could teach him to fetch you your outdoors shoes, Gran! Then you wouldn't have to go and look for them."

"Hm!" said Gran. "If Punch is going to be as clever as that, he will be a busybody! I think it would be better to teach him to wipe his feet on the mat when he comes in from a walk – that really would be something!"

"Woof." said Punch, sitting up straight, proud that he was being talked about. He gave Nick's hand a lick, and then Uncle Bob's. He did so like this family of his! He gave a happy sigh, and laid his head down on Uncle Bob's foot.

"He's getting a bit soft," said Nick, amused. "Biscuit, Punch?"

Punch stopped being "soft" at once, and sat up, barking.

"Beg, then, beg properly!" ordered Nick, and waited for Punch to sit up on his hind legs, front paws waving in the air.

"Not very steady, are you?" said Nick, and gave him a biscuit.

It was really good to have Uncle Bob in the house. He was always ready for a joke, always ready to give a hand with anything, and full of funny stories about his work, though, of course, he never gave any secrets away. He took Punch for long walks, he went shopping for Nick's mother, and was quite one of the family.

But there were times when he sat silent by the window, drawing on his pipe, hardly answering anyone who spoke to him.

He puzzled Nick and Mike particularly one rainy morning. They were full of high spirits, and wanted him to join in the fun, but he seemed somehow far away, and didn't even notice when Punch tried to leap on to his knee.

Nick went to his mother. "Mum, is Uncle Bob all right today? He's hardly spoken a word."

"Well, I told you he's been overworking," said his mother. "He's been forbidden to do any of his work for a while, and the days must sometimes seem empty to him now that he has no puzzling cases or problems to work out. With a brain like his, he must often be bored to death, not being able to use it. I only wish something interesting would happen, so that he could have something to think about."

"What sort of thing do you mean?" asked Nick. "Burglaries, or kidnappings – something like that? I bet our policeman would be proud to have Uncle Bob's help if anything happened here. But nothing ever does, unless you count things like Mrs Lane's washing being stolen off her line, or somebody breaking the baker's window!"

"No, of course I don't mean things like that," said his mother. "I don't really know what I do mean, except that Bob needs something to take his mind off himself. It's not like him to sit around, feeling so depressed. I think the doctor's wrong. Bob doesn't need time on his hands like this, he wants something to do, something to set those brains of his working again, instead of rusting."

It was unusual for his mother to confide in him. Nick stared at her, worried. "Would he like to go bird-watching with us?" he said, hopefully.

"Well, you ask him. See what you can do," said his mother. "He can't bear me or Gran to fuss round him, and I hate to see him sitting there not taking any notice of anything, as he's doing today! Maybe you and Mike can help him more than anyone else can."

Nick went off with Punch, looking thoughtful. Poor old Uncle Bob! He certainly must miss the exciting life he usually had, tracking down criminals, perhaps hunting a murderer, or finding stolen goods! But what could he and Mike do to help?

"Come on, Punch, we'll find Mike and see if he's got any good ideas," said Nick. Off they went to Mike's house, little knowing what a good idea Mike would have, and what extraordinary things would come of it!

Chapter 5

Mike has an Idea

Mike was down in his shed as usual. Penelope was there too, cleaning some garden tools.

"Hello, Mike!" said Nick. "Hello, Penny!"

Penny didn't answer.

"She wants to be called Penelope now," explained Mike. "She won't answer to Penny."

"Oh," said Nick astonished. "But why? Penelope is rather a silly sort of name – Penny's much nicer."

"Well, if that's what you think, I'll go," said Penny huffily. She promptly threw down the hoe she was cleaning, and went.

"Good!" said Mike, with a sigh of relief. "She's been reading an old Greek story about some amazing woman called Penelope whose husband went away to battle while she ruled the country. Now she thinks her full name is wonderful! Any news?"

"Yes. A bit," said Nick. "I want your help, Mike. Stop messing about with those mice."

Mike looked serious at once, and shut the door of the cage. "What on earth's up?" he said. "You look as solemn as Penny!"

Nick began to explain about his godfather. "Mum thinks he's depressed," he said. "You know, misses his work. Hasn't anything to sharpen his brains on. She said that perhaps you and I could think of something interesting to brighten him up."

"He might like my mice," said Mike at once. "They're really interesting. This one, now, he washes his whiskers just as if—"

"Don't be silly, Mike. Who wants to sit and watch mice washing their whiskers? I'd go crazy if I'd nothing better to do than that! No, I mean something really exciting, something to take the place of all the interesting and complicated puzzles and problems that Uncle Bob has to solve for people, when he's in London."

"Well, let's make up a few for him," said Mike, half joking. "Let's see now. 'The Mystery of the Lights in the Empty House' or 'Who is the Prisoner in the Cave?' or

'What Made Those Strange Noises in the Night?' It would be a bit of fun for all of us! We'd lead him properly up the garden path!"

"You really are an idiot, Mike," said Nick. "You know we couldn't do things like that."

He drummed his heels against the side of the box on which he was sitting. Then he suddenly stopped, and sat up straight. He gave Mike a delighted punch and stared at him with bright eyes.

"Now what's up?" said Mike, quite surprised.

"Well, it's just that I think you've got hold of a good idea," said Nick. "It sounded too stupid for words when you said all that but, you know, there's something in it!"

"Woof." said Punch, feeling Nick's sudden excitement and putting his paw up on the boy's knee.

"You don't mean we could make up a mystery for your godfather to solve, do you?" said Mike disbelievingly. "He'd be wild when he found out! Anyway, he'd never believe in it. He'd smell a rat at once."

"Woof!" said Punch again, hearing the word "rat".

"Don't interrupt, Punch," said Nick, feeling more and more excited. "Mike, it would be fun! We'll work out something between us. Let me see – how could it be done? I'll have to think."

"Look – we can't deceive your godfather like that," said Mike, really alarmed now. "He'd be furious. Anyway, he's so clever he'd see through it at once. We can't pit our brains against his!"

"We can try!" said Nick, scarlet with excitement. "Look, something like this, Mike. We'll get him to come out bird-watching with us, taking our binoculars, of course. And we'll put clues in different places for him to find."

"You're crazy," said Mike, disgusted.

"I'm not. We could let a piece of paper blow in the wind, and when he picks it up, he finds it's a message in code! Ha, very mysterious! And we could get him to train his binoculars on something peculiar, and—"

"Peculiar? What do you mean, peculiar?" asked Mike, puzzled.

"Oh, someone signalling out of a window or out of that old tower up on the hills!" said

Nick. "I'm sure Uncle Bob would think that peculiar, and he'd want to find out what was going on."

"Yes, but actually there wouldn't *be* anything going on," said Mike. "And he'd soon find that out."

"Oh, shut up finding fault with every thing I say," said Nick, drumming his heels angrily against the box and making Punch bark again. "I thought you'd be glad to help. Mum said we might think of something together, and here you've come up with a fantastic idea, that would be fun for all of us – and now you pooh-pooh it! I only wish I'd thought of it!"

Mike began to think he must have been very clever after all. He stopped making difficulties. "Oh well, if you really think I've had a brainwave, I'll help. But it's all got to be worked out carefully, mind, this pretend mystery, whatever it is. And what will your uncle say when he finds it's all a hoax?"

"He'll laugh like anything," said Nick. "He's got a terrific sense of humour and he never minds a joke against himself. We'll be giving him a bit of excitement, something to puzzle over and stop him thinking about himself. And what's more, we'll enjoy it too! Won't we, Punch, old thing?"

Punch hadn't the faintest idea what the boys were talking about, but he heartily agreed with everything. He ran round the shed, barking loudly, and nosed excitedly into every corner.

"He's looking for a deep, dark secret, a hidden mystery that only Uncle Bob can solve," said Nick, in a hollow, dramatic voice that made Mike laugh, and Punch look up in surprise.

"All right," said Mike. "You think up the clues. I thought of the idea, so I've done my bit. Is all this to happen in the daytime or at night? I'm quite game to wander about at night, if you want me to. Only it's no good asking Mum if I can, she'd say no."

"Mike, you mustn't say anything about this to your mother!" said Nick in horror. "She'd go and tell my mother at once, and that would be the end of it. We're doing this to help Uncle Bob, remember, and nobody except you and me must know about it. And Punch, of course."

"When will you think out the clues we're

going to spread around?" asked Mike. "I'm beginning to feel excited."

"I'd better think about them in bed tonight," said Nick, sliding off the box. "That's when I get my best ideas. What a laugh we'll have! By the way I'm teaching Punch some tricks. Like to come and help? I'm teaching him to fetch people's slippers for them. He's already got the hang of it."

"Really? Isn't he a marvellous dog?" said Mike, twiddling one of Punch's sticking-up ears. "Yes, I'll come. And listen, Nick, don't say a word of our plan in front of Penny – Penelope, I mean – you know how inquisitive she is."

"As if I would!" said Nick scornfully. "Come on, Punch. Come and show us what a clever dog you are!"

And, for the next half-hour, Nick's house echoed to sounds of "Fetch it, then, boy! Gran's shoes! Up the stairs, Punch! That's right. He's gone to get one, Mike! Go on, Punch! Granny's shoes!"

Down the stairs came Punch at top speed, carrying one of Uncle Bob's bedroom slippers in his mouth. He put it down at

Nick's feet with a look of pride, his tail wagging nineteen to the dozen.

"Idiot!" said Nick. "I said Gran's, not Uncle Bob's. Try again." And up the stairs went Punch, tail down now. He appeared in a few seconds with one of Nick's football boots, tripping over the laces on the way.

"He's not really very clever, is he?" said Mike.

Nick was puzzled. "I don't understand him. He fetched Gran's shoes after breakfast all right."

A voice came down the stairs – Gran's. "Nick! Please stop Punch scratching at my door. He can't have my shoes – I'm wearing them!"

"There!" said Nick, relieved. "I knew there was a good reason why he didn't bring them. Good dog, Punch. You can help us with our secret plan! You're as clever as a bagful of monkeys!"

Chapter 6

Nick Makes Some Plans

For once Nick went off to bed without voicing his usual strong objections. He was longing to think up some wonderful mystery for Uncle Bob! Gran was surprised when he kissed her so early in the evening.

"My, Nick – you're going early tonight!" she said, "Are you feeling all right?"

"Yes, I'm fine," said Nick. "I just want to think something out in bed, that's all. 'Night, Mum, 'night, Dad. Come on, Punch."

Punch leapt up, gave everyone a goodnight lick, and disappeared out of the door with Nick.

"Well! Nick usually watches that sports programme!" said Mum. "He must be very tired indeed."

He wasn't! He was very wide awake, and his mind was already busily thinking about plans as he undressed. Punch was surprised that Nick said nothing to him, for usually he was very talkative. He whined, thinking he must be in disgrace for something, but still Nick took no notice!

Punch wondered what to do. Why didn't Nick talk to him as he usually did? What had he done wrong? The little terrier suddenly barked and ran out of the room, his tail wagging. He knew how to please Nick and make him talk to him! He came back with a shoe of Uncle Bob's. Nick didn't even notice! Punch ran out again, and came back with Mum's bedroom slippers, and set them down beside the shoe. Then off he went again for more!

But Nick was still lost in thought. He had cleaned his teeth, washed, done his hair, and then, by mistake, he cleaned his teeth again without even noticing! That really did surprise Punch!

Nick leapt into bed, and was just about to put out his bedside light when he caught sight of the seven or eight slippers and shoes that Punch had been fetching to try to please him. There they were, all set out on the bedside rug, with Punch lying forlornly with his head on two of them.

"Oh, poor Punch!" said Nick. "I've not said a word to you for ages! I've been thinking hard, Punch, and all the time you've been rushing about fetching shoes to please me. Good dog! Did you think I was cross with you, or something? Well, I'm not. I think you're the best dog in the world!"

Punch went quite mad with joy. He tore round and round the room, sending the shoes flying, barking loudly, and then with one final enormous leap he landed on top of Nick, and licked every inch of his face.

"Oooh, Punch, that was my tummy you jumped on!" groaned Nick. "Lie down, you silly dog. No, you can't get into bed beside me. You know Mum will find you when she comes up, and you'll get a smack. Hey, look at all those slippers and shoes, honestly, you're crazy! Now just you take them back!"

But that was a trick that Punch had not yet learned, and he lay still, licking Nick's hand every now and again, glad to find that his beloved master was not angry with him at all.

"Now, just keep absolutely quiet," said Nick. "I'm going to have one of my thinking sessions, and I'll push you off the bed if you so much as wriggle your tail."

Punch lay so still that Nick forgot all about him, and was soon lost in thought. Now then – a really good mystery was what he wanted, complete with clues, strange goings-on, and all the rest of it. A mystery in which he could make Uncle Bob so interested that he would forget all about being bored and miserable.

Where should the mystery be? That was the first thing to work out. At once a picture of an old burnt-out building up on Skylark Hill came into Nick's mind. Yes, that would be a fine, eerie sort of place for a mystery. He thought about it, remembering the blackened, half-ruined walls with the one old tower still standing, the curious spiral stairway of stone that led down into the old cellars, which he and Mike had so often longed to explore.

"Mmm, yes, that's the place for a pretend mystery," thought Nick, beginning to feel excitement welling up inside him. "Now, what next? Clues. They'd better be in code,

an easy code, so that Uncle Bob can decipher it and read the message. And there should be lights signalling from the tower at night, Mike can go up there with his torch and flash it. And what about noises? If I can get Uncle up to the burnt house, Mike can hide and make awful groans. Wow, this is going to be great! If only I could tell Mike this very minute!"

He debated whether to put on his clothes again and slip over to Mike's. No, he'd probably be in bed, and if he was asleep nothing in the world would wake him, not even stones rattling against his window!

Nick became so excited as he thought of the wonderful mystery that was lying in wait for Uncle Bob that he couldn't keep still. He turned over and over in bed, and Punch was soon tired of continually being bumped. He leaped down to the rug, landing on the slippers and shoes.

"We'll begin the mystery tomorrow," thought Nick, sticking his hot feet out of the bed to cool them. "Ow, stop it, Punch! Those are my toes you're biting! Shhh, here comes Mum. Get under the bed."

Punch disappeared at once. Mum opened the bedroom door, and the landing light shone into the room, showing her Punch's surprising collection of shoes.

"So that's where my slippers went to!" she thought, and picked them up. "Heavens! This is quite a shoe shop! I'll have to stop these new tricks of Punch's, I can see!"

She laid her hand gently on Nick's forehead, for she still felt puzzled about his going off to bed so early. But it was quite cool and Nick was obviously all right! Picking up a few more shoes, she crept out of the room.

Punch came out from under the bed, and climbed carefully up beside Nick. He gave his face the tiniest lick, heaved an enormous sigh of love, and settled down to sleep.

Nick gave Punch a pat, and then slid off into his mystery once more. But now he was getting sleepy, and his thoughts became muddled. He was at the old burnt-out house and he was climbing up to the tower. A light was flashing there, no, two lights. Wrong! They weren't lights after all, they were the brilliant green eyes of Mike's cat which was growing simply enormous. Nick fled down to the cellar, where immediately a blood-curdling caterwauling broke out that made his hair stand on end!

He was so scared that he tried to scream, and immediately found himself sitting up in bed clutching at a growling, most surprised Punch.

"Oh, it was only a dream!" said Nick thankfully. "I suppose those awful noises I heard in my dream were you snoring or something, Punch. Phew, I was scared! If our mystery's going to be anything like as exciting as my dream, we're in for some fun. Get off my feet, Punch. No wonder I found it difficult to climb up to the tower in my dream, you must have been lying on my feet all the time!"

Punch obligingly slid off Nick's feet, and lay at the bottom of the bed. His ears twitched as an owl hooted somewhere in the trees at the bottom of the garden. They twitched again, and a small growl came from him when he heard a cat miaowing below the window. Nick turned over and buried his head in the pillow. He felt wide awake again, and longed for tomorrow to come so that he could tell Mike all his plans.

"Ha, Uncle Bob – you don't know what thrills I've got in store for you!" he murmured. "I'll write out that code message first thing tomorrow and show it to Mike – I bet he won't be able to decipher it! And we'll go up to that old burnt-out house and snoop round. I wonder what will come of my Plan for a Mystery – I do hope it will be a success!"

Chapter 7

A Mysterious Message

As soon as Nick woke up the next morning he remembered his wonderful plan of the night before. He sat up in bed, excited, and Punch began to pull off the bedclothes, trying to make his master get up and dress.

"All right, all right, Punch! I'm in just as much of a hurry as you are!" said Nick. "If Mike's up I could go and tell him my plans before breakfast. No, don't drag the pillow on to the floor. Bring me my shoe! Shoe, idiot, not boot."

Nick was soon dressed, and leapt down the stairs with Punch just in front. They almost bowled over Mrs Hawes, who was vacuuming the hall.

"Are you two catching a train or something?" she demanded. "Stop it, Punch, leave my vacuum cleaner alone! Nick, he's got my duster now. If he goes off with it, I'll—"

"Bad dog," said Nick sternly. "Drop it at once! There, see how obedient he is, Mrs Hawes. Do you know what's for breakfast? I've got time to go and see Mike, haven't I?"

"It's croissants for breakfast, and you've about ten minutes," said Mrs Hawes. "Bless that dog, he's gone off with my floor cloth now!"

Nick grinned and shot off at top speed after Punch. He ordered him to take back the floor cloth.

"And then come down to Mike's shed," he said. "But don't bring any shoes with you. I'm sorry I taught you that trick now."

He squeezed through the hedge and went across to Mike's shed. He could hear him chanting his favourite tune. Good, he was there then. He whistled piercingly and Mike at once appeared at the shed door, holding one of his smallest mice.

"Hello! You're early!" he said. "Anything up? Get down, Punch, you are not going to have mice for breakfast."

"Mike! I've thought out a smashing mystery!" said Nick. "Where's Penny? Not in hearing distance, I hope?"

"No. She's still in bed, reading. She's looking forward to Katie coming back today. But why are you up so early?"

"Because I wanted to tell you about the mystery I've thought out, the one we're going to pretend is a real one, so that Uncle Bob can have something exciting to think about," said Nick. "Honestly, Mike, it's really good, I tell you, we're going to have such fun. Let's shut the door and the window first. Punch, sit by the door and bark like mad if you hear footsteps or whispering."

Punch at once sat down by the door, and cocked his ears.

"Now we're safe," said Nick. "Listen, Mike."

And he told his surprised friend all that he had thought of during the night. Mike listened, gaping, taking in all the details, but when Nick came to the bit where he, Mike, was to go to the old burnt-out house at night and flash a torch, he shook his head firmly.

"No. If anyone's to do that, you can. I'd be scared to do that on my own."

"Oh, don't make things difficult," said

Nick. "Anyway, we can decide all the details later on. I just had to let you know what I'd planned. The first thing to do is to write out a secret message, in code, of course. Then we'll take Uncle Bob for a walk up Skylark Hill, and let him find the paper with the message on, and – oh blow! There's Mum calling me for breakfast. You be thinking out a good secret message. I'll be back after breakfast."

He tore off with Punch barking at his heels, and just managed to be sitting down at the breakfast table before his father arrived.

"You seem out of breath," said his mother, surprised. "Have you been for a walk?"

"No. Just to see Mike about something important," said Nick. "Do you want me to do anything this morning, Mum? I thought I'd ask Uncle Bob if he'd like to go for a walk up on Skylark Hill with me and Mike. We want to go bird-watching, and Uncle Bob said he'd lend me his binoculars."

"I'm sure he'd love to go with you," said his mother, pleased. "It's such a beautiful morning, it will do him good, and he's always been so interested in birds. Then Katie should be back home by lunch-time and he'll be pleased to see her again and hear all her news."

Uncle Bob arrived a few minutes later, looking rather gloomy.

"Hello, everyone!" he said. "No, no croissants for me, thanks. I don't feel too good. Couldn't get a wink of sleep because of a barn owl screeching all night."

"I never heard it," said Nick's mother. "Poor old Bob, you do look washed out."

"Uncle Bob, come for a walk up Skylark Hill this morning!" said Nick, eagerly. "Mike's going too – bird-watching. We might see the sparrow-hawk. You said you'd lend me your binoculars, remember?"

"Right. I'll come with you," said Uncle Bob. "Do me good to stretch my legs. What time do you want to start?"

"Er – would ten o'clock do?" asked Nick, remembering that he must leave himself enough time to work out a message in code, so that he could plant it somewhere for Uncle Bob to find.

"That'll suit me fine," said Uncle Bob. "I'll find my binoculars after breakfast, they're still in one of my bags. Is Punch coming with us? I hope he won't race about and scare all the birds for miles."

"Of course he's coming," said Nick, feeling a sudden little paw on his knee. He bent down to Punch, who was as usual under the table. "You heard what Uncle Bob said, didn't you, Punch? No racing about and barking, but plenty of sit and stay when you're told. Got that?"

"Woof," said Punch, quite understanding, and lay down again.

Nick hurriedly finished his breakfast, trying to think out what message he should write on a piece of paper.

"Please may I get down, Mum?" he asked. "I've a few things to do before we go."

"Well, remember that one of them is to make your bed, please," said his mother, as Nick raced off with Punch just behind him.

He went into his bedroom and hurriedly pulled his bedclothes back on to his bed. Then he tore a piece of paper from an old writing pad, sat down and chewed the end of his pencil. What should the message be? Perhaps he had better go and see if Mike had thought of one.

Soon he was down in Mike's shed. "Mike, I can't think of a message!" he said. "And Uncle Bob will be ready to go with us at ten. What shall—?"

"Don't worry. I've thought of one," said Mike proudly, and showed Nick a piece of dirty, torn paper. On it he had written a most mysterious looking message, which looked like this:

UFMM KJN XFSF SFBEZ. NFFU JO DFMMBST. TUVGG IJEEFO PO TLZMBSL IJMM. MPPL PVU GPS TJHOBM GSPN UPXFS.
IBSSZ.

"What on earth does that mean?" said Nick.

"It means: 'Tell Jim we're ready. Meet in cellars. Stuff hidden on Skylark Hill. Look out for signal from tower. Harry.'," said Mike proudly. "It's an awfully simple code. All I've done is to use the next letter to the real one each time, B for A, C for B, D for C and so on. This first word UFMM, for instance. All you've got to do is to think of the letter before ..."

"Oh, I see. For the letter U the one before would be T, and for F would be E, and for MM it would be LL," said Nick. "The word is 'tell', and so on. Isn't it too simple?"

"No. Don't you think it's an exciting message?" said Mike. "I mean, when your uncle picks up this dirty-looking bit of paper with such a strange coded message on it, he's bound to prick up his ears! I rubbed it on the floor of the shed to make it look dirty."

Nick began to feel excited. "Yes, it's fine!" he said. "I don't know how you thought of such an exciting message. That's brilliant, Mike. Look! When Uncle Bob is training his binoculars on some bird or other, you drop the bit of paper nearby, and maybe he'll see it and pick it up. If he doesn't I'll pick it up, and pretend to be very puzzled, because of the code. I bet Uncle will decipher it at once."

"And then the fun will begin!" said Mike, his eyes shining. "We'll go exploring the cellars, we'll hunt on the hill for the stuff that's supposed to be hidden there, we'll—"

"We'd better get moving!" said Nick. "It's almost ten, and I'm not ready yet. Meet me at your front gate as soon as you can. This is going to be fun! I bet Uncle Bob will prick up his ears and forget about feeling depressed once he gets going on our mystery!"

Chapter 8

Up on Skylark Hill

Nick and Punch raced off to see if Uncle Bob was ready to go for the walk up Skylark Hill. Yes, there he was, waiting impatiently in the front garden, his binoculars slung round his neck.

"Oh, there you are," he said. "Where's Mike?"

"Just coming, he'll be at his front gate," said Nick. "Shall I go in and get my bird book, Uncle?"

"No. I can tell you anything you want to know," said his godfather. "For heaven's sake, let's start while it's fine! Come along."

They picked up Mike at his front gate and set out happily; Mike had his binoculars slung round his neck just like Uncle Bob. They came to Skylark Hill, and at first took an ordinary path, Punch running ahead as usual, sniffing about for rabbits.

The birds were singing madly. "There's the chaffinch, with his 'chip-chip-cherry-erry-eery-chippy-oo-EEE-ar' song," said Uncle Bob, standing to listen. "And you can hear that greenfinch, and the yellow-hammer. And what's that now, singing so very loudly?"

"The wren. Look, it's over there!" said Mike, pointing. "Seems funny that such a little bird should have such a very loud voice!"

It was lovely up on the hill. It was quite a wild part where they were now wandering, no paths at all, except for those made by the rabbits. Uncle Bob suddenly stopped.

"Listen! There's a skylark singing high up in the sky. Take my binoculars, Nick, and see if you can spot it. There aren't so many about nowadays, so we're lucky to hear one."

"I've got it," said Nick. "It's only just visible even with binoculars. It must be very high."

"Nick, look over to your right," called Mike. "There's the sparrow-hawk. He's just circling lazily, looking for his lunch."

"I wonder where the barn owl that kept me awake last night sleeps," said Uncle Bob. "It might be fun to go out one night and watch for it as it grows dark. There are not so many of those about now, either."

Nick at once gave Mike a violent nudge. What a wonderful excuse for coming out at night! Perhaps he could make Mike go up unseen to the old tower and flash his torch, while he and Uncle Bob were watching for owls! Uncle Bob would never guess that the flashing light was a put-up job, he would be sure to think there was something funny going on in that old burnt-out house! He'd smell a mystery at once!

They went on a little way, and soon Nick thought it was about time that Mike dropped his dirty piece of paper with the coded message on it. He nudged him again, and Mike put his hand in his pocket, and nodded.

He went on some way in front, and suddenly spotted a chaffinch's nest in a bush. Ah, now he could perhaps make Nick's uncle find the paper for himself! That would be very much better than either he or Nick pretending to find it. He cautiously parted the twigs, and dropped the note into the bushy part below the nest. Then he called to Nick.

"I say, here's an old nest. Ask your Uncle Bob what kind it is, it looks like a chaffinch's to me."

Uncle Bob and Nick came up the steep little rabbit path. They peered into the bush. "Yes, that's a chaffinch's nest – see how neat it is," said Uncle Bob. "The bird has even woven in tiny bits of torn paper below the nest."

And, much to the boys' delight, he picked up the note that Mike had just dropped into the bush. He saw that something was written on it and glanced idly at it, as he was about to screw it up.

"Hello, what's this? It's a note written in code!" he said in surprise.

"Wow!" said both boys at once, pretending to be astonished. "Code! What does it say?"

"Don't know, unless I can break the code," said Uncle Bob. "It looks a fairly simple one. See what you can make of it. I don't feel too bright this morning."

The boys didn't know whether to decipher it or not. Wouldn't Uncle Bob think they were a bit too clever if they did? They sat down and put their heads together, pretending to puzzle over the strange message.

"Look at that first word," said Uncle Bob. "U-F-M-M. A double letter at the end. Now, what letters can be doubled at the end of words? S can, for instance. There are plenty of four-letter words ending in double S – fuss, boss, toss, hiss and so on, or in double F – such as huff, muff, etc."

"Or double L," said Nick. "Like ball, call, toll, er..."

"Or 'tell'!" said Mike, as if he had just that very minute thought of it. "It might be 'tell', mightn't it?"

"I should think it's more likely to be 'tell' than anything else," said Uncle Bob, taking back the paper. "Now, let's see what the next word would be, if the first is 'tell'. It will mean that the letters of each code-word must be replaced by the preceding letters of the alphabet. All right, the next code-word is K-J-N. We'll replace those three letters by the alphabet letters immediately before them. That is, K would be J, J would be I, and N would be M, making the word J-I-M, Jim!"

"Aha!" said Mike, "that would make the first two words 'Tell Jim'! You've broken the code already! We'll be able to decipher the whole message now!"

He looked so excited that Nick stared at him in surprise. How clever Mike was at acting! No one would ever think that it was he himself who had actually made up the message and put it into code!

Uncle Bob looked rather startled. He stared at the message again, and stood frowning over it.

"Strange!" he said at last. "That's the code all right, a very simple one too. Listen, I'll decode the whole message."

The boys felt a great desire to giggle. This was marvellous! Uncle Bob was well and truly taken in! They listened as he slowly read the decoded message.

"'Tell – Jim – we're – ready. Meet – in – cellars. Stuff – hidden – on – Skylark – Hill. Look – out – for – signal – from – tower. Harry.'"

He frowned down at the paper again. "Why did the writer of this message, whoever he is, use such an easily deciphered code?" he wondered. "He might just as well have written it in plain English! I wonder if it could be a joke, but if so, how did it come to be in that bush?"

"Perhaps the wind blew it there," suggested Nick. "Oh Uncle Bob, it's really exciting, isn't it?"

Uncle Bob put the paper into his pocket. "Something funny about it," he said. "Funny and phoney! I'll have to think about it."

"Should we try and find whatever stuff it is that's supposed to be hidden on the hill?" said Mike, feeling nervous in case Uncle Bob should decide it was a hoax. "We might find something interesting. Stolen goods, or – or hidden money, perhaps."

"And what about looking in the cellars of that old burnt-out house?" suggested Nick. "It says something about cellars in that note, doesn't it, Uncle Bob? It might mean the old cellars up in that place on the top of the hill. And it's got a tower too, a fine tower to signal from!"

"Yes, anyone on the hillside waiting for a signal could easily see flashes from that tower!" said Mike, backing up Nick valiantly. "Listen! We can see that tower from our back gardens, you know – we ought to watch out at night, in case someone does signal!"

"Well, I must say it all sounds rather odd, and I can't help feeling there's something wrong – something false – about that note," said Uncle Bob, frowning. "It's too easy a code. I'll think about it. In the meantime, what about a little more bird-watching?"

"Let's go to the old burnt house," suggested Nick. "It's quite interesting, Uncle. The tower is still all right – and the cellars too, though most of the walls have fallen down."

"Well, we'll have a quick look round," said his godfather. "But I'm pretty certain that note doesn't mean a thing, probably some silly schoolboy joke. Still, I can see you're longing to do a little exploring, so come along!"

The two boys fell behind Uncle Bob, as he went up the hill. "Do you think he suspects us?" said Nick in a low voice. "You heard what he said about 'a schoolboy joke'."

"Yes, but I don't believe he thinks we wrote that message," answered Mike. "Come on, it will be fun to explore that old place again."

"Punch! You can't possibly get down that rabbit-hole," called Nick. "Come along, we're going up to the old cellars and you'll love sniffing round those! You might even find a rat!"

Rat? Ah, that made Punch leave his rabbit-hole at once, and tear after Nick. He hadn't any interest in birds and there didn't seem to be any rabbits about, but maybe a nice big rat would turn up in those old cellars. Woof!

Chapter 9

"Loomy and Gloomy, Glowering and Towering!"

Nick led the way up to the top of Skylark Hill, following the overgrown path that had once been used by the people who had lived in the great building at the summit. They came to a gateway, where broken gates hung all askew on their hinges and the old drive that had led to the house was now a mass of strong-growing weeds.

"What a miserable-looking place!" said Uncle Bob. "It gives me the creeps."

"Wait till you get a good view of the burnt-out building," said Nick. "That'll give you nightmares!"

They went up the thickly-weeded drive

and past a great clump of pines. Behind these, sheltered from the prevailing wind, stood the great blackened hulk that had once been a grand mansion, overlooking the countryside with majestic splendour.

Uncle Bob stopped. From the bottom of the hill the old building had merely looked a tumbledown skeleton, its one remaining tower outlined against the sky, but here, at close quarters, it was rather frightening.

"It sort of looms over you!" said Mike.

"Yes, I know exactly what you mean," said Uncle Bob. "It frowns, and glowers, and, as you so rightly say, looms."

"It's loomy and gloomy and glowering and towering, and sulky and hulky," said Nick, most unexpectedly.

Uncle Bob and Mike stared at him in amazed surprise. "Why, that's poetry!" said Mike. "Surely that didn't come out of your own head?"

"Well, it did," said Nick, almost as surprised as the others.

"Whether it came out of your own head or not, it exactly describes this brooding, desolate old ruin," said Uncle Bob. "You might give us a warning when you're going to break out into verse again, Nick. I feel almost as surprised as if Punch had suddenly burst into song!"

"Woof!" said Punch, pleased at hearing himself talked about. He ran on in front of them, his tail wagging. He had been here before, and thought it was a most exciting place.

They all went up the curving drive, and came to the great building itself. It was a sorry sight. The fire that had devoured it had swept it from top to bottom, and had left only one tower untouched, though blackened with smoke.

"Birds build nests in the tower now," said Mike, as they went towards the fallen archway that had once framed the great front entrance. "And once I saw a badger coming out of a hole in the wall."

"Who lived here?" asked Uncle Bob. "It must have been a wonderful place."

"Somebody foreign," said Nick, trying to remember. "A very wealthy man who came from Egypt, I think."

"It had a magnificent view!" said Uncle

Bob. "I wonder what caused the fire."

"Nobody knows," said Mike. "The people down in the valley woke one night to see flames reaching up into the sky – and not a single fire engine could get up this hill to do anything to help. The building just burned to a shell. Everyone in it escaped, and went back to Egypt. The wealthy owner – who was a prince of some kind – never came back."

"The house was full of amazing treasures. There was even an Egyptian mummy!" said Nick. "Maybe that's what caused the fire – the curse of the mummy!"

"I don't think a curse was responsible for this fire," said Uncle Bob, with a laugh. "More like an electrical fault, I expect."

"People are scared of coming up here," said Mike. "It's a bit spooky. Anyway, let's go in. We can show you the cellars, at least."

"Yes, we'd better, as the writer of that peculiar message, what was the name he signed now? – Harry – mentioned something about cellars, didn't he?" said Uncle Bob.

He walked into what must once have been a great hall. The floor was still paved with stone, though it was now cracked

and blackened, and weeds grew up in the crevices. Nick pointed to a burnt mass of wood hanging from one of the walls.

"That was one of the staircases," he said. "But the tower had a stone stairway, so it wasn't burned. A good many of the steps are damaged, though – perhaps the heat cracked them. Some of them are missing, so you have to be careful climbing up."

He led Uncle Bob to a far corner of the old hall, and through a small stone-arched doorway. "Here's the tower!" he said. "And that's the stone staircase up to it, going up round the walls. Not very safe, is it?"

"Have you ever been up?" asked Uncle Bob, going up the first few steps.

"Oh, yes!" said Nick. "There used to be an iron rail fixed into the wall. There's still some of it left, so you can hang on to that when you come to the broken-away bits."

Uncle Bob began to ascend the narrow stone stair. He went very gingerly indeed, for much of the stone was breaking away, and he didn't want to plunge downwards. The boys followed.

When they came at last to the top, and

were able to look out of one of the great square stone windows through which the wind blew cold and strong, Uncle Bob gave a low whistle.

"My word! What a view! All round the hill, and down into the valleys for miles and miles."

"What a place to signal from too!" said Mike, giving Nick a nudge. "Flashes from this tower could be seen for a long way, couldn't they?"

"Yes, this would make a good place to signal from. But I don't imagine that anyone would want to come all the way up to this windy tower to do a spot of signalling that hundreds of people could see, if they happened to be looking!"

"I say, look, there's a dead match on the floor here," said Nick suddenly, and picked one up. "Would that belong to some signaller, do you think?"

Uncle Bob laughed. "No! To some innocent sightseer like us, I expect! Anyone would think you really do believe that message! I tell you, I'm pretty sure it's phoney, just a silly schoolboy joke."

"Where's Punch?" said Mike, hurriedly changing the subject. "Didn't he come up with us?"

"No, he doesn't much like the noise of the wind up here," said Nick. "Don't you remember how scared he was before, when we brought him up and the wind whistled all round him? He shot down again so fast that he rolled down the last dozen steps, and then sped off down the hill at sixty miles an hour! Let's go down and find him. He'll be lonely."

So they left the magnificent view and went carefully down the stone staircase, calling to Punch as they came near the bottom. But no answering bark came, no patter of eager feet.

"*Punch!*" yelled Nick. "Where are you? Surely you haven't gone home without us?"

Not a sound was to be heard, except for the hoarse croaks of crows flying around the tower. Punch was nowhere to be seen!

"Where on earth has the idiot gone?" said Nick, puzzled. "Can he have gone down the spiral staircase to the cellars? Not without us, surely?"

"Where is this spiral staircase?" asked Uncle Bob, looking all round.

"In the kitchen part of the building," said Mike, and led the way through a great doorway, one side of which had fallen in, through a passage, and into what must have been the kitchen, for old iron stoves still lined the walls.

The boys called loudly as they went.

"Punch! *Punch!* Where are you?"

"Here's the cellar door," said Mike. "At least here is where it used to be before it was burned off its hinges!"

A narrow stone doorway led into an equally narrow passage. Nick produced a torch, and shone it before him. "Better go carefully, Uncle," he said. "These steps are pretty steep, and slimy too, because they're rather damp. See how they go round and round in a spiral?"

It was indeed a curious spiral staircase, and dangerous too. Uncle Bob wished there was a hand-rail to hold on to! At last, after treading warily down what seemed to be at least fifty curving stone steps, they reached the bottom.

"What a horrible place!" said Uncle Bob, shivering. It was pitch-black, cold and rather smelly. "Surely Punch didn't come down here?"

But he *was* down there! From what seemed to be a great distance, his bark came echoing up to them, sounding weirdly hollow – and scared!

"PUNCH! Come here! PUNCH!" shouted Nick.

But Punch didn't come. Only his bark came to their ears, a frightened pleading bark. What was the matter?

"Come on. I'm going to find him!" said Nick, and flashed his torch around, to see which was the best way to go. "Something's happened to old Punch. He sounds quite lost. I must go to him!"

Chapter 10

A Bit of Excitement

"Wait a minute!" said Uncle Bob. "Do you know your way around these cellars? It seems a pretty vast place down here, from what I can see by the light of your torch. Passages leading off everywhere! We might easily get lost."

"Once we find Punch he'll lead us safely back to the spiral staircase," said Nick. "Listen – he's barking again."

They went along a dark, low-roofed passage and came into yet another cellar, heaped with old rubbish. The fire had not reached down into the cellars, so the old boxes and junk had not been burned. And then, just at that moment, Nick's torch went out! They were in complete darkness.

"Battery's gone," said Nick in disgust. "If only Punch would come to us, and show us the way back! *Punch*! *Come here*!"

But no Punch came – and what was almost worse, he stopped barking! Not a sound came up the dark passages, and Nick felt scared. What could have happened to make Punch stop barking?

Uncle Bob took matters in hand at once. He took Nick firmly by the arm, and pushed him back towards the way they had come. "No more nonsense," he said. "If we go down there any further in complete darkness, we'll lose our way, and not know how to get back."

"But I can't leave Punch by himself," protested Nick, trying to wriggle away from his godfather's firm hand.

"If he went down there, he can come up again," said Uncle Bob. "Anyway, we are all going back at once! I'm a bit afraid we'll miss our way even the short distance we came, it's so dark. Mike – are you there? Keep close to us."

"I'm just behind you," said Mike, who felt only too thankful to be going back.

At last they were up in the kitchen again having found the spiral staircase very difficult indeed to climb in the darkness. "Whew!"

said Uncle Bob, sitting down hard on the wide window sill that ran round the great kitchen. "Whew! I don't particularly want to go down there again!"

Nick was almost in tears over Punch. He spoke sullenly to his uncle.

"I think we're cowards, leaving Punch down there. What are we going to do about it?"

"We'll wait here for a bit and see if he comes back by himself," said Uncle Bob. "If he doesn't we'll go home and get more powerful torches. But I don't think we need worry. Punch will appear soon."

Uncle Bob got up and wandered about a little. The boys sat sulkily on the old stone sill, ears open for Punch, eyes on the entrance to the cellars.

Suddenly Nick leaped to his feet. "I can hear Punch barking! Listen!" But the barking wasn't coming from the cellars! It came nearer and nearer. Mike looked out of the empty window-arch, and gave a shout.

"He's coming up the drive. Look, there he is, absolutely filthy! Punch! *Punch*! Here we are!"

Punch gave a delighted volley of barks, raced into the old building, and hurled himself on Nick, smothering him with dirt and licks. Nick hugged him.

"Where have you been, you dirty little dog? We thought you were down in the cellars."

"He was," said Uncle Bob. "And as he certainly didn't return up the spiral stairway, like we did, how on earth did he get out?"

"Down a rabbit-hole?" suggested Mike. "I never heard of any secret way out of the cellars. Must have been a rabbit-hole! You rascal, Punch! We almost got lost for good down those cellars because of you!"

Punch was hungry. He barked and tugged at Nick's sleeve, trying to pull him along. Nick patted him.

"All right, all right, we're all coming. I'm as hungry as you are! What about you, Uncle Bob?"

"Well, yes, I must say that for the first time since I came to stay with you, I feel really hungry!" said Uncle Bob. "We've certainly had an interesting morning. What with that rather strange coded message and all the birds we saw, as well as exploring this gloomy old building, I feel that life has become quite exciting again!"

The boys were pleased. They looked closely at Uncle Bob and decided that he already looked a bit more like the cheerful, amusing man he used to be.

"Our trick worked, didn't it?" said Mike in a low voice to Nick, as they went back down Skylark Hill. "But I wish your godfather believed more in that message of ours. I don't want our plan to come to a sudden end. It's been fun so far."

"The thing that puzzles me is how Punch got out of those cellars," said Nick. "I suppose he did find a rabbit warren and went through it and found a hole into the open air. But usually he's too big for any rabbit-hole."

"Well, what else could he have done?" said Mike. "I didn't much like going into those cellars. I couldn't help being glad there wasn't really any mysterious 'Harry' waiting down there to meet his men."

"Harry? Harry who?" said Nick, and then remembered the made-up message, and laughed. "Oh, of course, the Harry who was supposed to have signed that message! Well, Punch would have given him a bit of a fright, wouldn't he?"

Katie, Nick's sister, was standing at Mike's front gate with Penny, as Nick, Mike and Uncle Bob came up. Punch raced up to Katie, barking and jumping up, licking every bit of her he could find.

"Darling Punch! Please don't knock me over. I love you very much and I *have* missed you!"

"Hello, Katie! How lovely to see you again," said Uncle Bob, giving her a hug. "When did you get here?"

"I caught the twelve o'clock train and Penny met me at the station. We've been waiting for you all to come back. Sophie and David say 'Hi' to you, Nick."

"Oh, thanks," said Nick. "I hope we'll meet them again some time."

"I'm looking forward to talking to you, Katie," said Uncle Bob. "Nick has had me all to himself this last week."

"Oh, Uncle Bob, I'm sorry! I'm going to Penny's house for lunch," said Katie. "We're seeing a film this afternoon and then I'm staying the night."

"Oh, there'll be plenty of time to talk," replied Uncle Bob. "I'm here until after you go back to school."

"What have you been doing this morning, Mike?" asked Penny.

"It's a shame you weren't with us, Penny," said Uncle Bob. "We've had a really exciting time, what with finding a strange message in code hidden in a bird's nest and exploring that great ruined building up on Skylark Hill. Then Punch got himself lost in the cellars and we didn't know where he had got to."

"Oh, Uncle Bob, don't give away our secrets," said Nick in a low voice, horrified to think that the girls should be told all this. They were both agog at once, of course, and to the boys' despair and disgust Uncle Bob actually took out the coded message and showed it to the two excited girls.

"Oooh!" said Penny, her eyes big with amazement. "Is it a real message? Not just one made up by the boys? Once Mike did a message rather like this, and—"

"Shut up!" hissed Mike, and gave poor Penny such a hard pinch that she screamed and ran straight in through the gate, holding her arm. Uncle Bob stared after her in amazement.

"What's the matter with Penny all of a sudden?" he asked, but Katie, seeing Mike's grim look, decided not to say anything about the pinch. Fortunately, they heard Mrs Terry calling that lunch was ready and so Nick and his godfather walked smartly to the front gate and up the path, followed by an even more hungry Punch.

"It was mean of you to show the girls that secret message," Nick couldn't help saying to his uncle.

"What on earth's secret about it?" said his godfather, astonished. "Anyone might have found it! Anyway it's probably a hoax, so cheer up. There won't be any meeting in the cellars, nor will there be any flashing of signals in the tower. And I'm pretty confident there are no stolen goods hidden on the hill."

Nick frowned and set his teeth. "Oh, aren't there!" he thought. "You just wait and see, Uncle Bob! You'll be surprised! And very soon too! I'll just pay you back for showing our secret message to the girls! You just wait!"

It was a pity Uncle Bob couldn't read Nick's angry thoughts. He didn't even know that the boy felt so angry, or he would have been gentler with him. Poor Nick! He had only thought of the mystery because he wanted to help his uncle, and now everything had gone wrong. The two girls knew about the message and might spoil all their plans for cheering up Uncle Bob.

Nick was rather silent at lunch-time, wondering what to do next. Could he possibly persuade Mike to go and signal from the tower at night, so that he, Nick, could wake his uncle and tell him to look at the flashes. That would make him sit up and take notice! "It's no good me going to the tower," thought Nick. "Because some one has got to tell Uncle about the signalling, and he'd think it funny if Mike came to him in the middle of the night and I wasn't anywhere to be found. Oh bother! I do hope this plan isn't going wrong. Mike will simply have to go and do the signalling. He can take old Punch with him, if he's afraid. Yes, that's a good idea!"

"You're very quiet, Nick," said his mother.

"What are you thinking about so deeply?"

"He's puzzling over a very strange message, I expect!" said Uncle Bob, laughing. "Am I right, Nick?"

"No!" said Nick, so fiercely that everyone jumped, and Punch began to bark. "You wait and see, Uncle, I bet that message was right. You just wait and see!"

Chapter 11

Quite a Few Things Happen!

After lunch was over Nick disappeared.

"Where's he gone?" asked his mother. "He seems rather down in the dumps. What happened this morning, Bob?"

"Oh, nothing much," said Uncle Bob. "We did some bird-watching, found a strange message in a bush, explored that old burnt-out place and almost lost Punch in the cellars. Nick seemed a bit cross because we met Katie and Penelope, and I told them what we'd been doing."

"How silly of Nick to be cross about that!" said Mrs Terry. "But he and Mike can't bear Penny knowing about their doings. She's a bit of a snooper, from what I hear."

Nick was certainly feeling cross. After all

their trouble in making up a super mystery, Uncle Bob had laughed at it, and almost given it away! He made up his mind to go across to Mike's and find out whether Penny had wormed anything out of him. Mike wasn't very clever at keeping things from her.

Mike wasn't in the shed, but somebody was! Nick shushed Punch, afraid he would bark, and went to peep in at the window. Katie and Penny were there, poring over a piece of paper, and giggling.

What could be so amusing about it? Nick longed to know. Then a terrible thought struck him. Had the two girls found the first rough copy of that coded message? Had they looked in the drawer of the old table in the shed, where Mike kept his things? He ran up to the house to find Mike, and ask him where he had left the copy. If the girls knew all about their mystery, he and Mike might as well give up their little joke on Uncle Bob.

Mike was in his room, reading. He was very pleased to see Nick and Punch. "Hello! Anything up? You look upset," he said.

Nick told him what he had just seen.

"That annoying Penny!" said Mike, in

a rage. "I thought the girls were going into town, so I didn't bother to hide that first rough copy of the coded message. I was sure they'd do a bit of snooping sometime, but they said they were going out, so I didn't rush down to the shed to hide my things!"

"Well, we'd better give up the whole idea," said Nick, very angry. "And I just hope you keep Penny away from our things in future. Katie never interferes with my things!"

"What's Punch doing under my bed?" said Mike. "He's chewing my new slippers! Come on out, Punch, and behave yourself. Go down and chase the girls out of the shed."

Almost as if he understood what Mike had said, Punch ran to the door, pushed it open with his nose and disappeared. All right, if he couldn't play with Mike's slippers, he'd go and find someone else's. He wasn't going down to the shed! He slipped into the room that belonged to Penny and found the most wonderful collection of shoes of all kinds! He sniffed at a pair of fur boots, and settled down to chew them in peace and quiet.

The boys began to play a game of cards, but after a few minutes the thought of the two girls messing about in his shed was too much for Mike. "Let's go and give them a fright and turn them out," he said. "Come on." So down the stairs they went, and out into the garden. When they came to the shed, it was empty!

"Bother them! Where have they gone?" said Mike. "And where's the rough copy of that secret message? Here it is in my drawer. They'll pretend they never found it or read it!"

Punch arrived at that moment, carrying the fur boot he had been chewing. "Where did you get that, Punch?" said Nick sternly. Punch ran out into the garden with it, and Nick was just going after him when the two girls came running up to the shed, pretending to be very excited.

"Mike! Nick! What do you think we've found! A note! A secret message, just like the one you found up on the hills. See what it says. Let's decode it, quickly."

"We found it under a bush," said Katie. "Who could have put it there?"

"Idiots!" said Mike angrily. "You can't trick us!"

"It says we're to watch out for a man with a limp," said Penny. "And it's—"

"You made it all up yourselves and hid it, so don't tell such whopping stories," said Mike.

"Was your message true then?" asked Katie, giggling. "Go on, do tell us. We're certain you made yours up!"

Penny gave a sudden shriek, and pointed at Punch. "Katie! He's got one of my best fur boots! He's chewing it! Drop it, Punch, drop it!"

She made a dart at Punch, who picked up the fur boot and danced away with it, out of the shed. This was a lovely game! The two girls chased him up the garden and round the pond. Punch suddenly stopped and very neatly dropped the boot into the water, where it bobbed for a few seconds and then sank.

Penny angrily picked up a stick and ran after Punch, who at once disappeared through the hedge. "If you bring that dog of yours here again I'll – I'll put him in the dustbin!" she shouted. "He's ruined my new boot!"

"Have you been teaching Punch new tricks while I've been away?" Katie asked her brother. "If he starts chewing up shoes and running off with them, *we'll* get into trouble, not him!"

The boys decided to leave the two girls to rescue the boot and went through the hedge, grinning at one another. "Clever old Punch! The way he dropped Penny's boot into the water – just as if he were saying, 'Sucks to you! There goes your boot!'" said Mike. "Let's give him a big bone or something."

"There are some sausages in the fridge," said Nick. "I'll get him one if Mum is out of the way."

And a little later, a most surprised Punch was eating a really delicious sausage, and being patted and petted. Well! If dropping people's shoes into the pond produced sausages to eat, Punch was quite willing to drop any amount into all the ponds around!

Katie and Penny were quite determined not to make up their quarrel with the boys. "We'll just ignore them," said Penny. "Letting Punch drop my boot into the pond like that! They'll be telling him to drop our clothes in next and goodness knows what else. He's a most annoying dog!"

"He's a lovely dog really," said Katie. "Nick's been trying to train him to do all sorts of things and taking shoes must be one of them."

So, much to the boys' relief, the girls ignored them and said nothing more to them at all. They soon went off to the cinema to see a film, and afterwards they had fish and chips for supper in the cafe opposite the cinema. When they got home again, the boys were playing in Nick's garden, so the two girls watched television until bedtime and then went up to Penny's bedroom to read.

But that night something happened to make the girls change their minds about not speaking to Mike. They were both in bed, and had been asleep for some time, when the barn owl suddenly screeched outside. They both woke up with a jump.

"Blow that owl! It *will* sit in the tree at night below the window and screech its head off!" said Penny crossly. She jumped out of bed to frighten it away, and it flew off on silent white wings. Penny glanced idly out into the night. Her room was at the back of the house, and looked across the fields to Skylark Hill. Penny was just about to turn back to bed when something caught her eye. What was that flashing on the top of Skylark Hill? It must be a light in the old tower!

"It's those boys!" she said to herself. "Mike and Nick must be up there, playing a silly trick. That was one of the things in the so-called secret message we found in Mike's drawer – signals from the old tower! Katie, are you awake? There's a light flashing from the tower. Those boys must actually have gone up there to do what that silly message said!"

"But what on earth for?" said Katie, astonished. "Anyway, it's surely too late for the boys to be out, Penny. It's half past twelve!"

"I'll see if Mike's in bed," said Penny and went to the room across the passage, where Mike slept. She pushed open the door and switched on the light. To her amazement, Mike was in bed and asleep! Could it be Nick up in the tower, then, all alone? She shook Mike awake.

"What is it? What's up? Penny, what's the

matter?" mumbled Mike, sitting up, blinking and rubbing his eyes.

"Mike, there's a light signalling from the old tower on Skylark Hill," said Penny fearfully. "Just like you said it would in your secret message. Mike, can Nick be up there, all alone? If not – who is it?"

Mike shot out of bed and went into Penny's room. He looked through the window and had a real shock when he saw the flashes coming from the old tower up on the hill. He stared as if he couldn't believe his eyes!

"It can't be Nick!" he said, quite dazed. "He would have told me if he'd planned to do anything like that. Penny, there's something weird about this. There is really."

"That's what we think," said Penny. "We'll have to tell Uncle Bob in the morning. But I bet he won't believe us. He didn't believe that silly message of yours. It was a made-up one, wasn't it – all pretence?"

"Oh shut up!" said poor Mike. "I'm going to dress and go over to Nick's. I'll throw some stones at his window and try to wake him. If he doesn't come, I'll climb up the tree just outside and see if he's in bed. If he's not, he must be up in the tower. Whew! Rather him than me! I'd be scared stiff. Get back to bed, girls. I'll just drag on a few clothes, and I'll be off to Nick's."

In a few minutes' time, Mike was letting himself quietly out of the back door, and running down the garden to creep through the hedge. Would he find Nick in bed, or not? And if he was in bed, what in the world was happening up on Skylark Hill?

Chapter 12

An Adventurous Night

Mike was soon under Nick's bedroom window, which was at the front of the house. He scraped about in the gravel path there, and gathered a few small stones. He threw them up one by one, missing the window with all but two which hit the glass with a sharp click. Nick was fast asleep, and didn't stir. As a rule not even a thunderstorm could wake him!

But someone else stirred, someone who pricked up his ears at the very first sound. Punch was on Nick's bed as usual, and he growled when he heard the soft tread of footsteps outside. He growled even more when a stone struck the window! Then he gave a sharp bark, and pulled at the bedclothes which were tucked around Nick.

Nick woke up. "Shut up, Punch! What do

you think you're doing?" he said sleepily.

Punch tugged at his sleeve as he sat up, rubbing his eyes. *Click*! That was another small stone against the window. Punch growled again and ran across the room, standing up with his paws on the sill.

"Is there somebody out there?" said Nick, waking up properly now. He leaped out of bed and joined Punch at the window. "Anybody there?" he called.

"Shhh!" said Mike's voice from below. "It's me, Mike. I'm coming up the tree, Nick. Give me a hand at the top, will you? I've some amazing news!"

He climbed the tree carefully, which wasn't easy in the dark. Nick took his torch and shone it down the tree to give him a little light. Mike was most relieved when he was at last on the sill.

"What's up?" asked Nick.

"There's someone in the old tower, signalling," said Mike. "Penny's bedroom faces that way, and she saw them and came to wake me. At first she thought it might be us up there on the hill carrying out what we'd said in that coded message! Who on earth can it be? I did think for a moment it might be you, but I know you wouldn't go without telling me, of course!"

"Mike! This is extraordinary!" said Nick. "I mean, we go and make up a mystery, put in signals from the tower and it comes true! Look, are you sure that you saw flashes? You might have been half asleep or something."

"Well, I wasn't," said Mike. "Nor were the girls. Look, let's go into a room where we get a view of Skylark Hill and the tower – we can't see them from your window."

"Woof!" said Punch, annoyed because Mike and Nick were taking absolutely no notice of him. He was delighted to see Mike in the middle of the night, but neither of the boys had even patted his head! They were too puzzled and excited to fuss over Punch.

"Now you be quiet, Punch, and don't growl or whine or anything," ordered Nick, in a low voice. "Stay here for a minute. We'll be back soon."

He and Mike stole across the passage to an empty room at the back of the house but a tree stood right in front of the window, blocking their view.

"Bother," said Nick.

"Well, let's go into another room," said Mike.

"They're all occupied," said Nick. "Uncle Bob's got the spare room. We could creep into that if he's asleep. I daren't risk waking up Dad."

"Come on, then," said Mike. So Nick led him down a passage to another door. They listened outside. To their delight little snores came from the inside – Uncle Bob was well and truly asleep!

They turned the door-handle carefully, and crept in. A lamp in the street outside gave a faint light to the room, which had its curtains pulled right back. The boys avoided some clothes on the floor and tiptoed to the window, glad that the curtains were open. They pressed their noses to the glass, and looked towards Skylark Hill. Faintly outlined against the night sky was the old tower and, as the two boys watched, they saw a sudden sharp flick of light, then another and another.

"There you are!" said Mike in excitement. "See that and that! If that's not someone signalling I'd like to know what it is!"

The light from the streetlamp caught some glassy surface in the room, and Nick realised what it was.

"Look! Uncle's binoculars are over there in that corner. Let's borrow them and see if we can focus them on the tower and then we'll see more clearly what's going on!"

In his haste to get the binoculars, Nick fell over some shoes on the floor, and knocked against the bed. Uncle Bob awoke at once and the bed creaked as he sat up in alarm. "Who's there? What is it?"

"It's all right, Uncle Bob, it's only us – me

and Mike," said Nick.

Uncle Bob switched on his bedside light and stared at the boys in the greatest astonishment.

"What in the world are you doing?" he asked. "And what's Mike here for, in the middle of the night? Or am I dreaming?"

"Uncle Bob, listen!" said Nick, keeping his voice low. "Someone's signalling from the tower on Skylark Hill. It looks as if he's signalling with a powerful torch."

"Now look here, my boy, don't let's have any more of this silly nonsense," said Uncle Bob, annoyed. "I'm pretty certain you and Mike made up that coded message, the look on your faces gave you away! I didn't mind playing along with you for a joke but when it comes to you both invading my bedroom in the middle of the night, and talking about someone signalling from the tower, it's just too much!"

"Didn't you believe our message then?" said Nick, feeling very small.

"Look, I'm a private detective in real life, as you very well know!" said Uncle Bob. "And I'm not likely to be taken in by a joke invented by a couple of silly schoolboys. Now get out of my bedroom, and don't let's hear any more of this nonsense."

"But listen, Uncle Bob," said Nick desperately. "We *did* see lights in the tower and so did the two girls. Look, you get your binoculars and focus them on the tower. I bet you'll get as much of a surprise as we did."

"I simply don't believe a word of it," said Uncle Bob, reaching for his binoculars. "And I very much resent you two boys barging into my bedroom in the middle of the night and telling me fairytales!"

He got out of bed, picked up the binoculars, and went to the window. He focused the glasses carefully on the tower and stared for so long that the boys felt impatient.

"Can you see lights flashing?" asked Nick at last.

Uncle Bob lowered the glasses and turned to the two anxious boys.

"No!" he said. "There's not a thing to be seen. Just as I thought! You both deserve a good telling off for coming into my room like this at night. You really must think I'm a bit of a fool to play such idiotic tricks on me. Now get out, and be your age!"

"But Uncle Bob," began Nick desperately. "I tell you we did see some—"

"Oh shut up and go away," said Uncle Bob, and gave the boys a hard push. Mike wriggled away and went to the window for a quick look at the tower. Uncle Bob was right, all was darkness there now. Whoever had been signalling had stopped flashing his torch. What bad luck!

"Come on, Nick," said Mike, and the two boys went out of the room, dismayed and angry. Who would have thought that Uncle Bob would treat them like that?

The boys sat on Nick's bed, an excited Punch between them, and talked sorrowfully about Uncle Bob's utter disbelief.

"Anyway, there is something going on up there," said Mike. "And we'll go and find out what it's all about. We made up a mystery which seems to be coming true! That's strange, but strange things do happen."

"All right. We'll keep Uncle Bob out of it all," said Nick. "We'll solve everything ourselves. We'll take Punch up to the tower tomorrow and scout round for all we're worth! We'll show Uncle Bob we're better detectives than he is! But I do hope he doesn't tell Dad about all this. I'll get into big trouble, I really will."

"Cheer up, he won't say a word," said Mike comfortingly. "He's angry with us now for waking him but he's not mean enough to get us into trouble! I rather wish we hadn't made up that mystery now!"

"Well, I don't," said Nick. "If we hadn't thought of it, we'd never be solving this one, would we? You go back home now, Mike, and we'll talk about it tomorrow."

"The girls will be waiting for me," said Mike. "They're going to ask all sorts of questions."

"We'll have to tell them everything, Mike," said Nick. "After all, it was they who saw the lights flashing from the tower. I couldn't keep Katie out of things now."

"Oh, no!" said Mike. "That means I'll have to tell Penny. But they're not coming up to the tower with us, Nick. I won't have that! What we do, we do on our own."

"All right," said Nick, as Mike climbed

out of the window. "I'll leave you to argue with them about that. Bye, Mike! Sleep well and dream of adventures!"

Chapter 13

Exciting Plans

The girls were both fast asleep when Mike crept back to their room, so he didn't disturb them. He was, in fact, very thankful not to have to explain what had happened.

He went back to his own bed, puzzling about the lights in the tower for a few seconds, and then fell into a deep sleep. Penny woke him in the morning by shaking him violently, demanding to know whether it was Nick who had been up in the tower during the night, signalling with a torch.

"No, it wasn't," said Mike. "And get out of my room. Can't you wait till I'm dressed? I'll tell you everything then, though I don't really think you deserve to come in on this, after all your snooping."

"Oh, Mike – we won't snoop any more," said Penny. "But Mike, was that secret message of yours real, not made up? How did you know about the lights in the tower? I mean, you must have known something, to put that in the message, if you did make it up."

"You're muddling me," said Mike. "Do stop talking and let me get up. We'll have a meeting down in the shed after breakfast."

And so at ten o'clock Katie and Penny went down the garden to the shed to join the boys. Mike was already there, cleaning out his mice, and Nick had just arrived with Punch.

Nick took charge at once, determined not to let Penny argue with Mike or try to lay down the law.

"Now, just listen," he said. "You know that Mike and I made up a mystery to interest Uncle Bob, and make him forget about being depressed. Mike wrote out that message and put it into code, which was very bright of him, and we dropped it into the bush on Skylark Hill. That's where Uncle Bob found it, and he seemed to believe it, I must say."

"I bet he didn't really," said Penny, with a

giggle. "He wouldn't have shown it to us, if he'd really believed it."

"Shut up, Penny," said Mike sharply, and Penny subsided, a grin spreading over her face.

"Well," went on Nick, "you two girls saw lights in the tower last night, and told Mike, so he came over to me, and we both saw them. We had to go in to Uncle Bob's room to look, and he woke up, and—"

"Ooh! Did he see them too?" asked Katie. "Whatever did he say? I bet he believed in your mystery then!"

"No, he didn't see them," said Nick. "The signals had stopped by the time he had got to the window. So he doesn't believe us, he thinks we made up the flashing signals, and he's so angry that he won't listen to a single word about any mystery now, real or otherwise!"

"Oh no!" said Katie. "What are we going to do, then? I mean, your pretend mystery's turned into a real one, hasn't it? Someone must have been in the tower last night, up to no good, and there are others in the mystery too – the people he was contacting. And what was he signalling about, and why, and—?"

"All right, all right, Katie," said Mike. "Just be quiet for a minute and let Nick get a word in edgeways. It's only because you and Penny saw the flashes last night, and were decent enough to tell me, that we're letting you come in on this."

"And what's more we're going to tell you any future plans we make," said Nick. "You'll have to be in on this now that you know so much, but you've both got to take orders from me, and do as you are told, okay?"

"Right," said Penny, glowing with excitement. "Wow, Nick – you sound exactly like Uncle Bob. I'll do exactly what you say! You will, too, won't you, Katie?"

"I don't know about that," said Katie. "I'll back up the boys – but I'm going to have my say about things, too."

"WOOF!" said Punch, sitting up straight as if he thoroughly agreed with all this.

"Now don't you start airing your views, too," said Nick, giving Punch a tap on the head. "It's bad enough coping with two girls without you entering into an argument as well!"

That made everyone laugh. Mike went to his cupboard and took out a packet of toffees.

"All this talk is making me hungry," he said. "Have some, girls? No, not you, Punch. Have you forgotten what happened to you last time you chewed a toffee? You lost your bark for ages because your teeth got stuck together!"

Penny giggled. "Oh, I wish I'd seen him! Now, do let's get on with your plans. What are we going to do about this mystery? What do you think is going on?"

"Well, I really haven't the faintest idea," confessed Nick. "I've just thought of the usual things – you know, thieves, somebody captured and imprisoned up there, or someone hiding there for some reason, perhaps an escaped prisoner…"

"Great!" said Penny, her eyes gleaming with excitement. "Go on, Nick!"

"Whatever it is, we're going to find out," said Mike firmly. "And though we'll let you girls know what we're doing, you are not going to be mixed up in anything dangerous."

"We'll see about that," said Katie.

Mike put the toffee bag well out of Punch's reach, and sat down. "I think the first thing to do is to try and find out who was up there signalling last night, see if they left any traces and try to find where they were hiding. That means that Nick and I go up there for the day, taking a picnic lunch, and do a bit of spying."

"We ought to go down into the cellars again and look around," said Nick. "We couldn't look around properly yesterday because my torch battery went flat. There might be some very interesting clues down there!"

"You be careful, then!" said Penny. "But listen, I've just had a thought! Do you remember Jean, who used to come in and help Mum? Well, her sister is caretaker at the local museum here, and one day when we were there, she showed us some old plans of that burnt-out house made before it was destroyed, and you should have seen the plans of the cellars. They seemed to go halfway down the hill!"

"Really?" said Nick, sitting up at once. "Look, there's something you girls could do. Go and have a look at the plans and perhaps copy them very simply. See what else you can find out too. There may have been some secret hiding-place, for instance, that might still be there. Somebody must be hiding up there, I'm sure!"

"Okay," said Katie. "We'll do that this morning. We'll go now!"

She jumped up, and so did Penny. They felt very excited. This was a real mystery now, not a silly made-up one, and they were in it!

"Right. You go straight away," said Nick, pleased to think that the girls would not be able to track them up the hill and follow them to the tower, as he had been half afraid they might. They would be safe in the museum. He stood up. "I'll go and get some lunch for the two of us, Mike," he said. "Mrs Hawes is there today and she makes smashing sandwiches! I'll take some water and biscuits for Punch. That all right for you, Mr Greedy?"

Punch danced round him, delighted to hear Nick talking to him at last.

"Woof! Woof!" he said, and Nick patted him. Punch ran to Katie, and she patted him too.

"You'd better not ask Penny for a pat,"

she said. "She hasn't forgotten how you tried to drown her shoe yesterday!"

At the word "shoe" Punch was off like lightning. Nick groaned. "Why did you mention the word 'shoe'? I thought he'd forgotten all about shoes today, he hasn't dragged any downstairs at all. Now he's gone to fetch some, I bet you anything you like!"

He and Mike went back through the hedge to find Mrs Hawes, who was very pleased to make them sandwiches.

"That dog of yours shot past me at sixty miles an hour just now," she said. "Up to some kind of mischief, I'll be bound!"

And, sure enough, by the time the boys were ready to go, and the sandwiches were on the kitchen table, Punch had raided all the bedrooms and brought at least six pairs of shoes into the kitchen!

"You take them back!" ordered Mrs Hawes, pointing at them with the bread-knife. "If you think I'm going to trot up and down the stairs with all those shoes, you'd better think again!"

"Oh, you idiot, Punch!" said Nick, gathering them up. "This trick isn't funny any more! Mike, take the sandwiches and stick them in my rucksack, will you? And fetch some apples and bananas from the fruit bowl, and a couple of drinks from the fridge. I'll bring some chocolate and the biscuits and water for Punch, although he doesn't deserve them, messing about with everyone's shoes like this!"

Mrs Hawes heaved a sigh of relief when all three were safely out of the house, Punch barking with joy. He was off for the day with the boys, could anything be more exciting than that? Well, Punch, it may perhaps be a little more exciting than any of you imagine!

Chapter 14

The Cellars in the Hill

While the two boys set off to go up to Skylark Hill, Katie and Penny walked in the opposite direction to the little local museum.

"There's Jean's sister over there," said Penny, nodding towards a plump little woman who was dusting the glass-fronted museum cases. "Hello, Miss Clewes. How's Jean? I haven't seen her today."

"She's in bed with a cold, Penny," said Miss Clewes. "Well, it's not often I see either of you here. Last time I saw you was when you came with your school class to study some old documents about our village. What do you want to look at this morning?"

"Well, Miss Clewes, we're interested in the great old place up on Skylark Hill," said Katie. "The one that burned down years ago. Are there any plans of it?"

"Oh, yes, plenty," said Miss Clewes, bustling over to a cupboard. "Funny you should come about that old place. There's been quite a lot of people looking at the plans lately. But surely nobody would want to build that awful building up again, would they?"

"What sort of people came?" asked Penny, surprised.

"Well, not very pleasant people," said Miss Clewes, getting some enormous rolls of paper out of a cupboard. "Men, you know, very off-hand – almost rude, poring over these plans, and making notes. I said to them: 'What's the excitement about, all of a sudden? Thinking of rebuilding the old place and living there in style, like in the old days?'"

"And what did they say to that?" asked Katie.

"Oh, they said maybe they were going to do that, and maybe they weren't," said little Miss Clewes. "And that it wasn't any of my business! Quite rude, they were."

Katie and Penny immediately thought to themselves that they must remember to tell the boys about these unpleasant men who'd been looking at the maps of the old house.

Then they got to work and unrolled the enormous plans and studied them. It wasn't very easy to make out what the plans showed. The girls ignored the ones of the great house itself, because the fire had destroyed all the rooms, both upstairs and down, and only the stone walls were standing now.

"Are these the plans of the cellars?" asked Katie, poring over a curious map that showed what looked like passages and caves.

"Yes. The plans of the house itself aren't much use to anyone," said Miss Clewes, "but the plans of the passages and caves that honeycomb the hill are still more or less correct, I should think. The people who used to live in the old mansion used them as cellars, but they were natural cellars, if you know what I mean, not man-made; saved people the trouble of digging out cellars for the goods or food they wanted to store years ago."

"Are there any old stories about the place?" asked Penny.

"Well, a few, but I wouldn't pay much attention to them," said Miss Clewes, rolling up the plans the girls had finished with.

"It's said that the prince who owned the place had an Egyptian mummy among his possessions and that there was a curse on him for bringing it out of Egypt."

"Was it a real mummy in a beautiful painted mummy-case?" asked Katie. "We were learning about them in history last year."

"I don't know whether there really was a mummy or a mummy-case; it's just a story," replied Miss Clewes. "There were many strange and beautiful things in the house, I believe, and nothing was saved from the fire."

"How sad!" said Penny. "Do you mind if we quickly trace the map of the old passages and caves in the hill just near the burnt building, the ones used as cellars? We might go exploring there today."

"No, don't you do that," said Miss Clewes. "Since we had a great storm and a cloud-burst of rain five years ago, those underground places have been dangerous – fallen in, you know, or full of water. You'd much better not go exploring there."

"Well, we'll see," said Katie, putting a piece of tracing paper over the map of the cellars, and running her pencil here and there. "I'll let you know what happens if we do explore!"

The girls left the museum at last, taking with them a very well-traced copy of the passages and caves that made up the cellars of the old building.

"I don't expect it will be of any use," said Katie, "but you never know! It wouldn't really matter if the boys got lost in the cellars, because Punch could easily bring them out. A dog always knows the way! What shall we do now?"

"Well, I'm very hungry," said Penny. "Let's go home and get some sandwiches and apples, and go up on Skylark Hill. I know the boys don't want us spying on them, but we could just have a look round. We could sit and have our sandwiches on the hill, and listen to the birds singing, especially the skylarks, of course!"

So back they went to Penny's house and made themselves some ham sandwiches, and took some apples from the fruit bowl. Then they set off to Skylark Hill and found a cosy place at the bottom where they could sit and eat in peace.

"Let's have a good look at our map-tracing, too," said Katie. "I've an idea it might help us a lot. If only we could find the lower entrance to the cellars, it would save us going all the way up to the old building!"

It was very pleasant sitting in the sun, munching, and poring over the map. Penny folded it up at last. "I wonder what the boys have been doing," she said. "How I'd like to know! Let's have a walk up the hill, and see if we can spot anything interesting. We've been ages eating our lunch!"

The boys had had a most adventurous time. They had gone up to the old tower first of all, and examined it thoroughly, trying to find some traces of whoever had been signalling there the night before.

"Here's another match like the one we found before," announced Mike, picking one up from the stone sill. "This is the window-opening that the signaller must have used last night. And here's a second match on the floor, and an empty cigarette packet."

"Well, at least we know a real person was here," said Nick. "It wasn't just a ghost signalling!"

They made their way down the dangerous staircase, and Mike picked up yet another match. Then, down in the kitchen, they found an empty matchbox, thrown near the old iron stoves. They looked at the name on the matchbox.

"This is a very odd-looking matchbox! The writing's not in English, or even French. I wonder what it is?" said Mike. "There's only one word on it I recognise," he went on, "and that's 'Cairo'. That's in Egypt, isn't it? Perhaps the signaller's Egyptian! Now we know something about him! And we know he smokes these cigarettes, because he left the empty packet behind. He's not very careful, is he?"

"Why should he be?" said Nick. "He's probably only using this place to signal from, because any light can be seen for miles, and he'll be away long before daylight, I should think."

"He could hide quite well in those old cellars, if he wanted to," suggested Mike.

"Maybe. Yes, that's quite a thought. Or, somebody might be using the caves as a hiding-place for stolen goods, and the time has come for whatever's hidden to be taken away. You know, I think we've hit on something!"

"You mean valuables may have been stored away in those old caves and passages, maybe stolen some time ago, and the thieves arranged for a signal to be given when it was safe to collect the things. A signal from someone in the know?"

"Yes, something like that," said Nick, feeling suddenly very excited. "Well, this is very mysterious! We certainly must go and explore those cellars. I'm glad we've brought strong torches – and Punch. He'll bark furiously if there's anyone down there."

"Perhaps that's why he barked the other day," said Mike. "Maybe there was someone down there then."

"Yes. Wow, isn't this getting exciting!" said Nick. "What about going down now? There's nothing more to be seen here. I've got the matchbox and the cigarette packet. Come on! We'll go down the cellar stairs very quietly and tell Punch not even to growl!"

So once again the boys went underground

down the curious spiral staircase, into pitch darkness, Punch at their heels. Nick shone his torch cautiously around. They were in the same dark, low-roofed passage they had found themselves in the day before. They went quietly along it and came to the cellar they had seen heaped with old junk. That was as far as they had gone yesterday, for it was here that Nick's battery had given out and they had been forced to go back.

But now their torches shone steadily and brilliantly before them, making a path through the darkness. They stood listening, and Nick put his hand on Punch's collar to stop him running forward. Not a sound could be heard, and Punch gave a very small whine. He wanted to go on!

"All right, Punch, but go quietly and carefully," Nick warned him. "We don't know what's down here, nor do we know who may be hiding, so walk just in front of us, okay?"

They went silently through another passage where the roof became so low in one place that the boys had to bend double to get through. Punch was very good. He stopped whenever they did, walked very slowly, and kept his nose in the air sniffing for smells of animals or humans all the time.

They came to three caves, all running into one another and leading into another passage, a wide one this time. And then, what a surprise! They came to a cave piled with tins, boxes and cartons of all sorts and sizes. Nick shone his torch on them.

"Tins of meat, butter, bacon, cartons of cigarettes, packets – hey! What's all this?" he whispered. "Someone's been living here for a while. Look at all the empty tins and cartons, as well as all the unopened ones. This must be where that signaller lives!"

"Better go carefully then," whispered Mike. "He may be near."

They went down another passage, so narrow that it was hard at times to squeeze through. And then Punch stood absolutely still and gave a very small, deep growl!

The two boys hardly dared to breathe.

What was Punch growling at? Then they knew! A long-drawn-out snore came to their ears, and then another! Someone was there, someone fast asleep. Who was it?

Chapter 15

Deep Underground

The two boys stood perfectly still, Punch just in front of them, still growling softly.

"Shhh!" whispered Nick, and Punch stopped growling at once. "Take hold of Punch's collar, Mike, while I go forward a little."

Mike held Punch's collar tightly while Nick went cautiously forward. The passage curved just there, and Nick felt sure that the snorer was just beyond the bend. He put his head round, and there, in the little side-cave, was an enormous man, lying on his back, snoring. Beside him were the remains of a meal, taken out of tins.

Nick stared at him. He was dark-skinned and had a thick black beard. Nick thought he looked as if he came from the East – was he Egyptian or Indian – or perhaps

Iranian? What on earth was he doing in the underground cellars?

Then Nick saw crates of different sizes across the cave and, nearby, a workbench with carpenter's tools lying higgledy-piggledy beside pieces of wood. At one end stood a large table covered with bottles, bowls and brushes beneath shelves full of dirty-looking objects, while in the far corner was a spade, a crowbar, and a pick, as well as a couple of buckets. A peculiarly pungent odour seeped out of the place.

He crept back to Mike, and pulled him further up the passage, so as to be out of the sleeping man's hearing, should he wake.

"Something's certainly going on down in these cellars," he said. "There are all kinds of tools down there, a workbench as well, and lots of large crates. A foreign-looking man with a beard is snoring away near them. What can he be doing? Oh, and there's a strange sort of smell in there that I don't recognise."

"I don't know what can be happening," said Mike, puzzled. "Maybe precious things were stored here when that great old building was lived in – or taken down here for safety when the fire began, and hidden – and then perhaps forgotten."

"Or they might have been stolen when the fire raged," said Nick. "Maybe someone set fire to the old place on purpose, so that they could run off with some of the really valuable things. After all, it was a prince who built that place and if he was so rich he must have had some fantastic treasures."

"Yes, and he was Egyptian," said Mike. "You said that snoring fellow down there looks foreign? I bet it's someone who's been told where something is hidden in this hill!"

"Hey! That's just like what we put in our coded message!" said Nick, startled. "Don't you remember? We put 'Stuff hidden on Skylark Hill'. We never guessed how true it was!"

"And we put in about the signalling from the tower, too," said Mike. "That came true, as well! What was the other thing we put? Oh yes, 'Meet in cellars'! Wow, it looks as if that's correct, too. I say, it's all very peculiar, isn't it?"

"It is rather," said Nick. "I mean, we only thought of our silly message just as a joke, something to amuse Uncle Bob. I don't much like the way it's all coming true. It's just as if we'd foretold what was going to happen."

"Well, we can't stop it now," said Mike. "We'd better look out for this cellar meeting next – perhaps someone is coming to talk to that snoring fellow. We might overhear something interesting."

Punch began to growl again, and Nick tapped his head. "Shut up! No noise now, Punch. Someone else may be coming."

Nick was right! The boys suddenly heard a scraping noise as if someone was walking up a passage to where the snoring man lay in the side-cave. Then a man's voice spoke angrily. "Hassan! Always you sleep! Why are you not working? How many crates are packed and ready to go?"

The sleeping man had awakened with a jump. He growled something in a language that the boys did not understand. Then there came the sound of things being dragged across the floor, and the boys imagined that Hassan was showing the other man the packed crates.

"Did you find the case?" asked the visitor. "You said you had been told where it had been put."

Apparently Hassan answered no, for the second man flew into a rage, and shouted a string of words that the boys couldn't understand. Punch began growling when he heard the angry shouts.

His growl must have been heard, for the two men suddenly fell silent.

"What was that?" asked the first man in English.

"It may be Harry coming down the passage," answered the second man. "Last night he signalled from the tower to warn the others that the crates were ready for collection."

Mike gave Nick a sudden nudge. Harry! That was the name Mike had chosen when he had signed the secret message! This was definitely very weird. Harry! He must be head of this gang. Would he come?

"Hope he won't come down this way," whispered Mike. "We'd be caught then, between Harry and the others. Oh dear! I don't much like this!"

He fell silent and in the silence the two boys heard another noise. Someone was coming down from the old building above and coming down by the very same path that they themselves had taken. The boys hurriedly squeezed into a little side cave, pulling Punch with them. If only this man would go by without seeing them.

He would have done, but for Punch, who could not resist another growl, rather a loud one this time. The man stopped at once.

"What's that? Who's there?" he called roughly.

There was no answer, of course, and then Punch growled again, a deep, angry growl that rumbled all round the little cave. The man bent down and looked into the cave. He was a hard-faced man, with a black patch over one eye. He flashed a torch on the boys and the dog.

"What's this? Who are you? What on earth are you doing here?" he shouted. Then he yelled to the other two men, who were looking extremely startled. "Look! There's a couple of kids here! Didn't I tell you to keep watch and see that no one came down here?

You idiots! Just when everything is almost ready! We've only got that case to find now. I'll knock your heads together – didn't I tell you that—"

"It is all right, Harry," said the second man. "If it is only children, they can be imprisoned in a cave with a rock against the entrance. We shall be finished here very soon. I think by tomorrow, is that not so, Hassan?"

"Tomorrow will be too late," shouted Harry. "Someone may come hunting for these two kids just when we want to take out all the stuff. We'd better go and tell the other two blokes to come up and help carry the crates tonight."

He turned to the two frightened boys. "Well, you've got mixed up in something you didn't expect," he said, in a voice the boys didn't like at all. "We shan't hurt you, but you'll be imprisoned in a cave till we're ready to go. Come on out of there – we'll find another cave for you with an entrance we can easily block."

The boys made no move, and the man lost his temper. He dragged them both out roughly. Growling furiously, Punch went completely mad. He flew at the man and bit him hard on the left foot, right through his shoe! The man gave an anguished yell, and pulled off his shoe at once. His foot was bleeding through his thin sock.

The other two men came running up and

Hassan aimed a vicious kick at poor Punch. How he yelped! He ran to Nick at once, but he ran on three legs, because one of his hind legs was badly hurt by the kick. Nick picked him up and ran, with Mike close behind him.

The men stumbled after them. "Look, let's get into that narrow passage running off to the left. The roof's so low that I don't think the men will be able to squeeze through after us," panted Nick.

"Right," said Mike, and he squeezed in after Nick, who found it very difficult with Punch in his arms. In fact he had to put him down at the end of the narrow passage, because there he had to crawl on hands and knees, the roof was so low.

The men stopped and one of them laughed. "Couldn't be better! They'll be nicely boxed up in there. We only need to roll up a heavy stone, and they'll be imprisoned! Serve them right – and that dog, too!"

The boys heard the sound of the men tugging at a rock and then with a thud it was right up against the opening to the narrow passage, completely blocking it. But neither of the boys worried about that. It was poor, whining Punch they were upset about. They shone a torch on to his leg, fearing that it was broken.

Luckily, it wasn't, although it was badly bruised and bleeding. Nick hugged Punch lovingly.

"You brave little dog!" he said. "I'm glad you bit that man. Does your leg hurt very much? Poor old Punch. Where's my hanky? I'll bind up your leg, and hope it will be all right."

Punch licked him, and gave a tiny whine as if to say, "Don't worry! We'll be all right!" But would they be all right? Did the men really mean to leave them imprisoned? And if so, how in the world would anyone ever find them?

Chapter 16

An Astonishing Find

The two boys sat silently for a while, with their arms round Punch. How sickening to be caught like this! Then Mike remembered the food they had brought with them in the bag. He brightened up at once.

"Let's have something to eat," he said. "It's about lunch-time, and I bet Punch would like his biscuits! Sandwiches will cheer us up, too!"

They certainly did! After the boys had eaten half the sandwiches, they felt very much better. They had a banana each too, and Punch had a biscuit and some water. Then they had one of the cans of drink.

"Better not eat everything now," said Mike. "You just never know how long we'll be imprisoned here."

"Not a good thought," said Nick. "Well,

anyway, the girls know we've come up here, so if we don't appear for some time, they'll tell Dad, and he'll organise a search party. Wait, though. What about trying to move that stone that they've put at the entrance to this place? We might be able to do it."

They crawled down the passage to the entrance. It was completely blocked with a very heavy rock indeed. No amount of shoving would move it. Punch came along and looked too. He began to scrape round the stone with his front paws, and managed to make a small space between the stone and the rocky entrance.

But it wasn't nearly big enough for either of the boys to squeeze through, try as they would. However, Punch managed to wriggle out, and set off cautiously on three legs down the passage where the men had gone.

"Be careful, Punch!" called Nick. "Come back before you get into any more trouble." Punch went on very carefully, giving a little growl every now and again. If only he could find those men, what a fright he would give them!

He came to the cave where Hassan, the

sleeping man, had been. No one was there. Punch sniffed round and came across one odd shoe. It was the shoe that Harry had removed from his swollen, bleeding foot, and thrown down in the cave of the crates when he had hobbled back after imprisoning the boys.

A shoe! Punch couldn't resist picking it up in his mouth and limping off with it.

Back he went to the boys' cave, shoe in mouth, proud of himself. Why, even down here he could show off his latest trick!

The boys couldn't help laughing when they saw Punch with the shoe in his mouth!

"Punch, you dear old idiot!" said Nick. "Where did you get that? Oh, of course, it must be the shoe that fellow took off when you bit his foot. Put it down, you clever dog! He can go without it and I hope the rocky floor hurts him!"

"Nick, do you think we can get out of the other end of this cave?" Mike said, shining his torch towards the back. "There must have been a fall of earth at some time, so if we dig through with our hands, we may find a passage we can get through."

"Right. Let's try," said Nick, bored with

doing nothing. So he and Mike and Punch all dug hard with hands and paws. The fall was very loose, and it was soon obvious that part of the earthy roof had caved in and blocked the passage.

"We're through the fall of earth!" said Mike suddenly, as his hand went through the last layer of soil into nothing. "Quick, we'll soon have a hole big enough for us to squeeze through. Punch wants to get out, he's almost through already. What's on the other side, Punch?"

Punch began to growl. He was on the other side of the earth-fall, and the boys couldn't see what he was growling at.

"There surely can't be any of the men there!" said Mike. "Here, let me wriggle through the hole we've made and shine my torch to see what's the other side. Punch must be growling at something!"

So Mike wriggled a little more, and was then able to shine his torch into the space beyond. He was silent for so long that Nick grew impatient.

"What is it? Can you see something?"

"Yes. Yes, I can certainly see something.

But I can't believe it!" said Mike, in an awed voice. "Nick – get beside me and look. I must be seeing things! It's so strange!"

Nick squeezed beside him and looked into the dark space lit by Mike's torch. He caught his breath in wonder and fear. Something very beautiful was there – something that looked at them out of glinting golden eyes, and glowed with colour from head to foot.

"What is it?" whispered Nick. "It looks alive but like something from another world."

"It is from another world," said Mike in wonder. "It's a mummy-case from Ancient Egypt. There's a picture of one in my encyclopaedia. I bet it's the one that belonged in the ruined house. Someone must have taken it down here for safety when the fire started."

"And stuffed it right at the back of the cave, and then a fall of earth came, and it was hidden from everyone's sight!" said Nick. "No one has found it since! We heard the second man asking Hassan if he had found the 'case'. They were talking about the mummy-case and we didn't realise. So, after all these years, somebody remembered, and

sent Hassan here to look for it!"

"I wish we had better light in here," said Mike, shining his torch on it. "The case is painted all over with little figures and birds and animals in blues and turquoises and oranges."

"The face looks almost alive with those golden eyes," whispered Nick, feeling quite awestruck. "Whatever happens, we mustn't let the men know it's here!"

"They're too big to get through that narrow low tunnel to it," said Mike. "We could only just squeeze through it ourselves. This is our secret, Nick! Hey, it's lucky we didn't put a mummy into our coded message, isn't it?"

"I do wish we could get out of here," said Nick. "There's rock behind the mummy-case so the passage must end there. Let's get back into the other part where there's more room. What a find! And to think it was all by accident that we spotted it! Come back, Punch!"

"What do you suppose the girls are doing?" said Mike, when they had gone back through the hole they had made and were sitting in the cave again. "I wish I knew where they were!"

At that very moment Katie and Penny were walking up Skylark Hill, excited because they had such a good tracing of the underground cellars in their hands. They were about halfway up when Katie stopped.

"Look! There's a strange man coming down the hill," she said. "He's foreign-looking with a very black beard. Isn't he tall?"

"And there's a second man with a black eye-patch," said Penny. "He's limping! He's only wearing one shoe and his foot's bleeding. And there's another man behind him who looks foreign, like the first man. Wherever can they have come from? They appeared so suddenly!"

"Penny, do you think they've come from the underground cellars?" said Katie. "We know how far down the hill they stretch, and we know there's an entrance at this lower end, as well as through the kitchen of the old house, and the boys told us that Punch must have found a way out, too. I think those men must have come from the same outlet that Punch found, when the boys missed him the other day. There's simply nowhere else on this hill for them to have so suddenly appeared from!"

"Oh, no, I think that one-eyed man is coming up to us," said Penny nervously.

Sure enough the man with the eye-patch limped up and spoke to them.

"I need a doctor," he said. "My foot's bleeding badly. It's been bitten by a dog. Can you tell me where there is a doctor, please?"

"Er – well, there's one down in the town there," answered Katie, pointing down the hill. "Anyone will tell you where he lives. Er – what kind of a dog bit you?"

The man didn't answer, but walked painfully back to the others. They set off down the hill again.

"I bet it was Punch who bit him!" said Penny. "I bet it was. Oh, Katie, you don't think anything's happened to the boys, do you? Hadn't we better go back home for help?"

"No. We'll try to find the place where the men came out of the hill," said Katie. "I think we ought to look for the boys and make sure they're all right. Come on, this way. That's where we first saw the men appear, over there. Quickly, Penny, the men may come back at any time."

The two of them hurried off, anxious and a little scared. There must be some way in to the caves, there must!

Chapter 17

The Girls are Very Clever

Katie and Penny made their way round the slope of the hill to where they had first seen the men appearing. They kept looking back over their shoulders to make sure that no one was following them.

"This is quite an adventure, Katie, isn't it?" said Penny excitedly. Then she gave a loud exclamation. "Oh! I've just thought of something."

"You made me jump!" said Katie, who was worrying about Nick and Punch. "What have you thought of?"

"That tracing we made of the underground cellars!" said Penny. "Let's have a look at it, and see if it will help us."

They sat down on the hillside and opened out the tracing paper. They pored over it, frowning.

"Look, here's the old building," said Penny, her finger on the map. "And here's where the cellars begin. They go along here, down under the hill of course, and spread out here and there – really underground passages, I suppose. But I don't see how we're going to tell where they come out on this part of the hill."

"Look, what's this on the tracing?" said Katie, pointing to a curving line. "Could it be a stream?"

"Well, I suppose it might," said Penny. "But what's the use of that? There's no stream here on the hill now, that I can see. It must have dried up years ago."

"But its bed will still be there like a dried-up ditch!" said Katie, jumping up. "Come on! If we can find that, and follow it uphill, we'll perhaps come across the bottom entrance to the cellars!"

The girls walked over to the place where they had first seen the three men appearing. They looked all round but saw nothing that could have been a stream-bed. Then Katie gave a shout.

"Here you are! This must have once been

a stream. It's the ditch running along this old hawthorn hedge."

"Yes, I think you're right," said Penny excitedly. She looked at the traced map again. "Here it is on the map," she said. "And look, it seems to go curving up the hill, and swings off just by where the entrance to the cellars is marked. Let's follow it!"

So the two girls went slowly up the hill, following the half-lost track of the old stream. But where could the entrance into the hill be found?

The old ditch took a sudden curve round, and Katie gave a shout.

"The entrance should be here, where the ditch curves. Look on the map and check it out, Penny. This is where we must hunt for the entrance, I'm sure!"

She was right. A great gorse bush barred their way, thick and prickly. The ditch curved round it, and Katie's quick eye saw a smooth patch of earth just under one side of the great bush.

"I think that's the way into the opening," she said. "See that worn patch of earth? The men may have gone in and out there. Oh no!

We'll be scratched to bits!"

They certainly did get very scratched! Luckily, they both had anoraks, and were able to wrap them round their faces and shoulders as they crawled under the prickly bush. Someone had cut away the bush in the thick middle part, so it was not so thorny there – and what a surprise they had!

A hole went down into the ground, almost under the middle of the bush; it had rough steps cut in one side. The girls crouched under the bush, and looked down into the hole rather doubtfully.

"Do we go down?" said Penny. "We don't know what's in there."

"Oh, come on. We must be brave!" said Katie, who was not feeling brave in the least. "I'll go first."

And down she went, groping with her feet to find the rough steps. Soon she was in an underground passage. She switched on the torch she had brought.

"Well, that was very clever of us," said Penny, jumping down and joining her. "Now, where do we go from here?"

"There's only one way, and that's up,"

said Katie. "It was lucky you took that tracing, Penny. Come on. I'll lead the way."

The two girls went slowly up the dark passage. They shone their torches into little and big side caves, marvelling at seeing so many. What a honeycombed hillside this was! There must have been many little underground streams at one time, rushing down to make such a number of caves and passages!

"Shall we shout and see if the boys answer?" said Katie. "There doesn't seem to be anyone here – no men, I mean. Let's shout."

So they yelled at the top of their voices. "Mick! Nick! Punch!"

The two boys, still sitting in their tiny cave, were too far away to hear anything. But Punch's ears were very sharp. He cocked them and listened. What was that far-off noise? He growled.

"Oh, don't say the men are returning," groaned Nick. "I'm fed up with them. What's the matter, Punch?"

Punch heard the far-away voices once more, and stood up on three legs, holding up his hurt one. He didn't growl this time. Surely he recognised those voices! He put his head on one side and listened hard.

The girls shouted again as they came up the underground passages in the hillside, and this time Punch knew the voices. That was Katie's voice, and that one was Penny's!

Punch barked loudly and joyfully, almost deafening the two boys in that small place. They stared at him in astonishment.

"What's the matter, Punch?" said Nick. "You're barking happily. Who's coming? It can't be the men or you'd be growling."

Punch gave Nick a quick lick and then limped to the rock and squeezed under it. He could hear the girls coming nearer and nearer and he barked delightedly. He went down the passage and found them. He tried to jump up at them but he couldn't with his bad leg so he licked them wherever he could find a place.

"Oh, Punch, what's happened to your poor leg?" cried Katie. "Did you bite that man? Where are the boys? Take us to them quickly!"

"We're coming, Mike. We're coming,

Nick," yelled Penny. "Where are you?"

"Here! Here! Can you hear us?" shouted Nick in delight, crawling as near as he could to the great stone that blocked the entrance. "Penny! Katie! Here we are – imprisoned in this cave."

Punch led the girls to where the boys were, and they called to them.

"We're here! We came all the way up from the lower entrance, the one Punch must have found the other day. We saw the men and they spoke to us!"

"Oh no! Did they see you coming up here?" asked Nick, as the two girls began to try and move the great stone from the entrance.

"No, they've gone down to the town to find a doctor!" shouted Katie. "I hope it was Punch who bit that man with the black eye-patch."

"It was," answered Mike. "Listen, we'll push this stone while you pull. It's such a weight that I doubt if even the four of us can move it."

To their enormous disappointment the great stone could not be moved even an inch!

It had taken three strong men to put it there, and four children were not strong enough to roll it away. It was most disappointing. Punch barked, and scrabbled frantically with his front paws, but it was no use. Everyone sat back to take a rest, and the boys told the girls about the mummy-case they had discovered in the hole behind the cave.

"Amazing! Miss Clewes at the museum told us about it!" said Penny. "No one has seen it, but there were stories about it and its curse."

"One of the men, the one called Hassan, had, I think, been told about the mummy by a friend. I suppose it was whoever hid it away when the fire broke out," said Nick. "Hassan was meant to be looking for it, but as they talked about a 'case' I didn't realise they were talking about the mummy-case."

"It's so beautiful," said Mike. "Just wait till you see it!"

"Anyway, what are we going to do now?" said Nick. "I don't like you girls hanging about in the passages in case those men come back. They might make you prisoners too."

"Would they?" said Penny, in alarm.

"Then hadn't we better go back straight away and get help? We could bring your Uncle Bob up here in no time, and your father, too!"

"Yes, I think you'd better do that," said Mike. "Don't you agree, Nick? But I bet Uncle Bob won't believe you! This mystery has come true in every detail in a most remarkable way. I'm never going to make up anything again!"

"We'll go now," said Katie. "Cheer up, both of you, and keep Punch with you for company. We'll be as quick as we can!"

And away went the two girls, very cautiously indeed. The boys sat silent, listening to the small noises they made as they went down the passage. Punch listened, too, his head on one side.

"Can't hear them any more," said Mike, with a sigh. "I'm getting tired of this hole, aren't you, Nick? I just hope the men don't come back. What do you suppose Uncle Bob will say when we show him the mummy-case?"

"Oh, he won't believe it!" said Nick, with a grin. "He-just-won't-believe-it!"

Chapter 18

Uncle Bob to the Rescue

The two girls went down the dark passage, their ears open for any sound of the men returning. Penny thought she heard a noise and stopped in alarm.

"Do you think it would be wiser to go up the passages to the old kitchen, and get out that way – the way the boys told us about?" said Penny. "It would be so terrifying if we met the men."

"No. Let's go on down," said Katie. "At least we know this way. The men won't be back yet. I expect they've not only gone to find a doctor but also to make plans for removing whatever they've hidden in the caves."

They came safely to the opening under the old gorse bush. It seemed to be more difficult getting out than getting in, and the girls were in a very dirty, untidy state when at last they were safely out of the bush, and standing on the hillside in the sun.

"Oh, it's good to be out in the open air and sunshine again!" said Penny, breathing in deeply. "I'm sorry for the two boys, shut up in that horrid little cave. Hurry up! Let's get back as soon as we can, and tell everyone where the boys are. Your dad's home today, isn't he? He can help your Uncle Bob. I don't know..."

"I wonder if Uncle Bob will believe our story," said Katie. "It does sound a bit weird, doesn't it – hidden men, caves, a mummy, the boys made prisoners. Still, strange things do happen – you read about them in the papers every day."

"Well, I never thought an adventure like this would happen to us!" said Penny. "Usually adventures are things that happen to other people. Come on, we're nearly home."

"I've been looking out for those men all the way back, but there hasn't been a sign of them," said Katie. "I'd run for miles if I did meet them!"

"We're back at last!" said Penny, as they came to Katie's front gate.

Katie ran into the house, calling for her mother and father. "Mum, Dad, where are you? Come quickly!"

"Your father's gone to the bank, and your mother's out shopping, Katie!" called Mrs Hawes from the kitchen. "But your Uncle Bob's in the garden reading the paper, if you want him."

"Yes, we do!" said Katie, and flew out into the garden, with Penny close behind. "Uncle Bob! *Uncle Bob!*"

"Hello, hello – what's all the excitement for, Katie?" said Uncle Bob in surprise. "And where are the boys?"

"Uncle Bob, something's happened," panted Katie. "The boys went up to the old burnt house this morning to find out about that signalling, and—"

"Now listen. I don't want to hear any more fairytales," said Uncle Bob, looking annoyed. "I'm tired of hearing what's in that silly message. I'm tired of the boys pretending that something's going on. The joke's over!"

"But Uncle Bob, the boys are prisoners

in a horrible little cave," said Katie, almost in tears. "A cave with a mummy at one end—"

Uncle Bob threw down his paper in exasperation. "What next! Do you really expect me to believe in a mummy in a cave in Skylark Hill? You must think I'm mad. Go away."

"The men have pushed a great heavy stone in front of the boys' cave," said Katie, in a suddenly trembling voice. "And Punch is hurt. One of the men kicked him. Oh, why isn't Dad here? I must get someone to help Nick and Mike. We saw those horrible men walking down the hillside, but I'm sure they'll soon be back. Penny, let's go and find your dad. He'll tell the police, I'm sure he will."

Tears suddenly ran down her cheeks, and Uncle Bob looked at her in surprise. He took her hand. "Katie, listen to me. Are you really telling the truth? This isn't just another idiotic bit of made-up mystery, is it? You remember the silly coded message I showed you about a meeting in cellars, stuff hidden on Skylark Hill, signals from the tower, signed 'Harry', and all made up by the boys? Well, are you sure this isn't another silly bit of nonsense?"

"It isn't nonsense. It's all true!" wept Katie. "It came true, I don't know how, but it did. And 'Harry' is one of the men. Uncle Bob, if you won't come up and help, I'll have to go and find Penny's dad."

"Well, this is about the strangest thing I've ever come across," said Uncle Bob. "How could a made-up mystery have any truth in it? All right, all right, I'm coming, Katie. Stop crying, both of you. I do believe you, though I'm blessed if I understand what's happening. Come along. We'll all go back to Skylark Hill."

So, much to the girls' relief, Uncle Bob hurried off with them to Skylark Hill. The birds were singing, just as they had been on the previous morning when he had gone there with the boys, but none of them stayed to listen. The girls were anxious to get back to the boys before the men returned and Uncle Bob was beginning to feel not only puzzled, but most disturbed. What in the world was going on?

The girls took him to the great gorse bush. "The entrance is right in the middle, a hole that goes underground," said Katie. "I saw the men coming from somewhere about here, so Penny and I looked at a map we have, and it showed an entrance just about here, too. So we hunted till we found it, but it's awfully prickly, Uncle Bob."

"Heavens, whatever next!" said Uncle Bob, not at all liking the idea of creeping under the great thorny bush, and sliding down underground. "Damn – I haven't brought a torch!"

"It's all right. We've one each," said Penny. "Do hurry, I'm so afraid the men will be back. And they're horrible, Uncle Bob!"

With many groans, Uncle Bob managed to get down the steps that led into the passage below. The girls switched on their torches, and at once beams of light cut through the darkness.

"This way," said Penny. "We can only go uphill and we pass lots of caves on the way."

Uncle Bob followed the two girls, wondering if he was dreaming! He saw the cave where the crates stood waiting to be collected. And then, in the distance, he heard a noise. He stopped.

"Wait, what's that?" he said.

"It's all right, it's only Punch barking," said Katie. "We'll soon come to the caves where the boys are. Who would have thought that the hill was riddled with passages and caves like this, Uncle Bob?"

As soon as Punch began to bark the boys wondered who was coming. Was it the men again? Surely it couldn't be the girls back with help already?

"Woof-woof-woof-woof!" barked Punch madly, scraping with his paws at the big stone blocking the cave entrance. He knew who was coming, he knew those voices as soon as he heard them far away in the distance, and he was under the rock and off to find them!

"Poor little Punch," said Uncle Bob, when Punch reached them, still limping. "He's got a nasty cut on that hind leg. Let's hurry to the cave and find the boys."

"Here we are," said Katie a minute later. "And there's the stone the men put in front, that we can't move."

"NICK! MIKE! We're here, and Uncle Bob's with us! You shove the stone and we'll tug it."

"Hello, Uncle!" shouted Nick in delight.

"Come on, now – all together!" And he and Mike shoved at the great stone with all their might, while Uncle Bob tugged and pulled till he was out of breath. The stone moved!

"It's coming!" yelled Penny, doing her bit too. "Shove again, boys! It's moving!"

The stone gave way so suddenly that the girls and Uncle Bob fell over. The boys crawled out at once, with Punch barking loudly and leaping round them all on his three good legs!

"Well!" said Uncle Bob, sitting on the ground, rubbing his grazed hands, for the stone was very rough and hard. "This is extraordinary, isn't it! I could hardly believe the story that the girls came and told me. And what's all this about a mummy?"

"Crawl into this cave, and you'll see a fall of earth near the end of it," said Nick. "Poke my torch through the hole in the middle of the fall, and see what's beyond!"

Uncle Bob did as he was told, though with much difficulty. When he saw the gleaming beauty of the magnificent painted mummy-case he was so amazed that at first he couldn't say a word.

"Well, what do you think about our pretend mystery now?" said Nick triumphantly. "We didn't put a mummy-case into it but everything else has come true!"

"I certainly have an apology to make to you all," said Uncle Bob, wriggling out of the cave. "This is a most incredible find. It's obviously the mummy-case that was somehow saved from the fire." He shook his head in astonishment. "And now I must go back to the cave I passed where there were lots of crates and see what's inside them."

They made their way to the cave of the crates and Uncle Bob looked round carefully. He went over to the table and looked at the bottles and tins there and sniffed them. Then he lifted the lid of one of the crates. He carefully unwrapped a heavy package. Inside he found a little golden figure.

"Look at this," he said. "It's a statue of the goddess, Isis, with her son Horus. It must have come from the tomb of someone very rich and important."

"It's beautiful!" said Katie, taking it from Uncle Bob.

Everyone crowded round to look at it.

Mike put a hand into the crate and pulled out a box full of painted figures of soldiers with shields and spears. "What are these?" he asked. "Do they come from an Egyptian tomb too?"

"I know what those are," said Penny, whose class had done a project on Egypt the previous term. "They're called shabti figures and they would have been placed in the tomb of a prince or a great soldier to fight for him in his after-life."

"Are these things real?" asked Nick. "I mean, are they very old?"

"Yes, they're real all right," answered Uncle Bob. "I can't believe it! We've been trying to find out how large numbers of Egyptian antiques are being brought out of Egypt and then sold all over the world. Now I understand how it's been done. Look over here." He led them to the table with bottles and brushes on it.

"Take this piece of jewellery and scratch it very gently, Katie," said Uncle Bob, taking a greeny-grey brooch from the shelf above the table.

Katie took the brooch and gently scratched

the surface. "Oh, look. There's deep blue underneath the grey – and here there's orange!"

"That's a beautiful antique scarab brooch, Katie," said Uncle Bob. "It's been painted with watered clay. It looks nothing now, just a cheap tourist trinket, but cleaned up it is worth a great deal of money. The precious things in these crates have been stolen from Ancient Egyptian tombs. Some are painted with a water-based gilt, some with water-based paint, or like this brooch, with clay – which doesn't harm the treasures and can be easily cleaned off. We knew that these things were being smuggled out of Egypt but we didn't know how or what happened to them after they left that country."

"So they're smuggled into England and are brought here to be cleaned – that's partly what the peculiar smell is, I suppose!" said Nick, red with excitement. "Then they're packed up, taken away and sold to collectors all over the world."

"And your three men are part of the smuggling ring!" said Uncle Bob. "This is the most extraordinary discovery. I must get on to the police at once! Come along, let's get back to the town. We mustn't lose any time. Those men will be back for the crates, though probably not till night-time."

Excited, chattering, thrilled to the core, the little party began to make its way down to the great gorse bush. They clambered up the hole one by one, and squeezed through the opening, pricked once more by the bush that guarded it.

And what did they see, as soon as they came into the open, but the three men straggling back up the hill! Harry had his foot bound up now, and was walking with a limp.

"There they are!" yelled Nick. "Look!"

At his shout the men stopped in surprise, then turned tail and ran off, Harry limping painfully down the hill. The boys were too stiff after their cramped ordeal to go after them, and the girls too scared. Uncle Bob grabbed hold of Nick in case he should take it into his head to chase them! Punch limped down the hill on three legs, barking, but soon came back.

"Let them go," said Uncle Bob. "The

police will round them up! You've done enough for one day. My word, what a shock those men must have had, when they saw us all crawling out from their own private entrance!"

Chapter 19

An Exciting Finish

Uncle Bob went quickly down the hill, followed by the four jubilant children. Punch hopped along behind on three legs, his left hind one still very bruised and painful. Nick turned round to make sure that he was following, and gave a sudden loud exclamation.

"Look! Look what Punch is carrying!"

They all turned, and how they laughed! Punch carried a shoe in his mouth, rather a large one with a bite right through the leather!

"It's the shoe belonging to Harry, the man that Punch bit!" said Nick. "Clever old Punch! You had to do your shoe-trick and bring a shoe along somehow. Drop it!"

"No," said Uncle Bob. "It might be useful. Let him carry it. Which man did it belong to?"

"Er – well, I'm afraid you'll think it's strange, but actually it belonged to a one-eyed man call Harry," said Mike. "The man whose name we put at the end of our secret message."

"How extraordinary!" said Uncle Bob. "I'm beginning to think that you and Nick must be in league with this band of thieves, or how else can you possibly know so much about them?"

Everyone laughed. It had been a very exciting two days and the made-up mystery had certainly cured Uncle Bob's depression. He was quite his old self again!

"That mummy-case really is a marvellous find, you know," said Uncle Bob. "There'll probably be a fine reward for that from the Egyptian owner, and you kids will get it!"

This was a most exciting thought! But there wasn't much time to consider it for they were now down in the town. Uncle Bob walked straight to the police station and asked for the superintendent. The children went with him, feeling very important.

The superintendent listened in amazement, for he knew Uncle Bob and his work very well. He took rapid notes, quickly telephoned somebody, called in three of his men and sharply rapped out some orders.

The children listened in excitement, but couldn't quite understand what was happening. The superintendent turned to them at last, and smiled.

"You've done some very good work!" he said. "I congratulate you. We shall have to ask you to identify these men for us, I'm afraid, once we've caught them, but we'll let you know when that happens."

"Yes, sir," said Nick delightedly. "And, er – what about the mummy-case, sir?"

"We'll see to that at once," said the superintendent, smiling. "Once we have it safely, we shall have to try and find the owner. He'll be delighted! But it's going to take a long time to sort out all the valuable things in those crates. Where did they come from? What is their value? What is to happen to them? I'm glad I won't have to do that job!"

"I'd love to help clean up some of those pieces that haven't been done yet," said Katie.

"That's a job for the specialists," said the superintendent, shaking hands with them all.

"Well, that's it for the moment. We'll let you know when we need you again, once we've rounded up the men."

"Punch is still carrying that shoe he brought from the caves," said Mike, when they were outside the police station. "Uncle Bob, ought we to leave it with the police?"

"No, let him take it home, and we'll wait till they ask us to go to the police station again," said Uncle Bob. "I don't expect it will be long before we get a call to go. I think that the superintendent had a very good idea where to look for those men."

Uncle Bob was right. The next day the police went to the next town where they had reason to believe that a small group of tourists had made their headquarters a few weeks back. They looked for the men that Nick and the others had described to them.

But not one of the men seemed to resemble the children's descriptions! There was no man with a beard, no man with a patch over one eye and all of them denied knowing anything at all about the old burnt mansion, or the caves in the hillside.

"Well, you will please come along with

us for an hour or two, for questioning," said the police officer, and hustled the men into a police van. A car was at once sent to the children's homes, with a message for them to go to the police station, and Uncle Bob, too. They piled into the car in great excitement. Punch went with them, of course!

The men were paraded in front of the four children. But what a disappointment! Not one of them seemed to be like the men they had seen underground, or those the girls had met coming down the hill! Not one had a beard – or wore an eye-patch.

But Punch recognised them! He growled and showed his teeth. He strained at the lead and tried to get at one of the scowling men.

"Sir!" cried Nick to the superintendent, "I believe that man is the one called Harry. He must have taken off the black eye-patch we saw him wearing. Punch bit right through his shoe and made his foot bleed, and he even carried home the shoe! The man couldn't wear it, because his bitten foot was bleeding and swollen. We've brought the shoe with us just in case it might be useful. Here it is!" And Nick promptly placed it on the superintendent's table.

The superintendent snapped out a few words, and the man sullenly took off his left shoe and sock. The foot was red and swollen, and teeth marks could plainly be seen. Punch gave a bloodcurdling growl, and the man edged away, scared.

"Put this other shoe on, the one the boy brought," ordered the superintendent. "See if it fits."

It did, of course, though the man pretended that he couldn't get it on!

"It's the same type of shoe that he's wearing now, sir," reported the sergeant who had been watching. "A foreign make, sir. Must be his!"

The man mumbled something angrily, and put on his other shoe again, easing it on gradually because the bite that Punch had given him was still painful. Nick noticed that his hands were shaking.

One of his friends noticed this too, and took out a packet of cigarettes. He offered it to the man, who took one thankfully. He was obviously in a state of panic.

Nick stared at the cigarette packet, and so

did Mike. It seemed somehow very familiar! Mike gave a sudden shout.

"He's one of the men too, sir – the one with the cigarettes."

"How do you know?" asked the superintendent, astonished.

"These cigarettes. We found an empty packet of them up in that old mansion!"

"Ah!" said the superintendent. "Got the empty packet with you?"

"Yes, sir," said Nick, and took out the packet from his pocket. "And we found an empty matchbox, sir – and these dead matches. I think they're Egyptian matches. I kept them in case they were clues!"

"Well, well, well!" said the superintendent, surprised, and he took them from Nick. "Search the pockets of these men, Sergeant, please."

The men stood sullenly while their pockets were turned out. Aha! Two of them had the same cigarette packets, and one had a box of similar matches to the ones the boys had picked up.

"There you are!" cried Nick, pleased. "This is the gang all right, sir. They were probably the signallers up in the tower and they smoked cigarettes and threw down the matches, and the empty box and packet. And the shoe belongs to that fellow who's called Harry. And I'm sure that the big fellow is Hassan. He's shaved off the black beard he had!"

"You know, Nick, you will be quite a help to your uncle, when you're a little older," said the superintendent, smiling broadly. "Take the men away, Sergeant. I'll deal with them later."

Uncle Bob, the children, and Punch went out, feeling very pleased with themselves. Uncle Bob stopped outside a shop.

"I think," he said, "that we should all go in here and celebrate the triumphs of that fine bunch of detectives, Nick, Mike, Katie and Penny – to say nothing of that remarkable hound, Punch, who knew when to turn a most annoying shoe-fetching trick into a wonderful clue. Punch, will you kindly lead the way? There can't be another dog in the world who can catch a criminal by the simple method of stealing his shoe!"

Everyone laughed. They trooped into the

shop, which sold the biggest and creamiest ice creams in the town. Uncle Bob promptly ordered two each.

"What – two for the dog as well?" said the shop-girl in amazement.

"Certainly! And bring six bottles of lemonade," said Uncle Bob.

"Lemonade for the dog, too?" said the shopgirl, quite dazed.

"Why not?" said Uncle Bob. "He likes lemonade so why shouldn't he share in our celebrations? Don't you agree, children?"

"Oh, *yes!*" said everyone, delighted that their little dog should be honoured. Punch barked joyfully, and ran round giving everyone a loving lick. He had quite forgotten his bad leg.

"Now, Uncle Bob, please explain again just exactly how those men stole all the things in the crates," begged Katie.

"Well, there are many precious old things found in Egypt which are often kept in warehouses after they have been dug up. It isn't hard to steal them and replace them with good fakes, but it is very difficult to get them out of the country and sell them abroad where collectors will pay high prices for them," explained Uncle Bob.

"So that's where the painting of them comes in?" asked Mike.

"Yes. That's what we didn't know before," said Uncle Bob. "But when I went into that cave, I realised how it was done. First, the antiques are covered with varnish and then painted to look like cheap tourist gifts. Then it was easy to get them through Customs and clean them up afterwards – that smell in the cave was the chemical used to remove the varnish."

The girl came back with a big tray full of ice creams and lemonade. Everyone eagerly set to. The ice creams were delicious. The lemonade fizzed and bubbled in the glasses. Uncle Bob raised his glass and spoke solemnly, with a twinkle in his eye.

"Here's to the 'Mystery-That-Came-True'! My congratulations to you all, and apologies for disbelieving you. And my grateful thanks for helping to solve a mystery that no one else could!"

"Hear, hear!" said everyone.

And Punch joined in too: "Woof-woof-

woof-woof!" What a time he had had! What an adventure!

"All the same," said Nick solemnly, "it's the very last time I'll ever invent a mystery. Honestly, I never guessed it would all come true! I'll be very careful in future, and so will Mike!"

No – don't be careful, Nick! Invent another one, and then tell us what happens!

Enid Blyton

RIDDLES SERIES

Follow the daring Nick and his sister Katie as they solve mysteries, elude kidnappers, discover hidden treasure, and much more.

The Riddle of Holiday House
9780753725542

The Riddle That Never Was
9780753725474

The Riddle of the Rajah's Ruby
9780753725559

Enid Blyton

RIDDLES SERIES

The Riddle of the Hollow Tree
9780753725610

The Riddle of the Hidden Treasure
9780753725627

The Riddle of The Boy Next Door
9780753725634

Enid Blyton
FAMILY ADVENTURES

Follow these families as they discover the joys and perils of growing up, find new adventures, and set the world to rights.

 **The Children at Green Meadows**
9780753725481

 **The Family at Red-Roofs**
9780753725580

 **Those Dreadful Children**
9780753725597

Enid Blyton

FAMILY ADVENTURES

The Put-Em-Rights
9780753725641

House at the Corner
9780753725573

The Six Bad Boys
9780753725603